## "What took the sheriff so long? Why did they spend so much time in her apartment?"

Uneasiness twitched through Ridge. He didn't want to face this.

"Ridge?" Sylvie prompted. "You're frightening me. What aren't you telling me?"

"Ginger's death has been deemed suspicious."

"Suspicious?"

"Her apartment had been ransacked."

"You mean someone broke in? Maybe you've got it wrong," Sylvie said.

Why couldn't she just accept what he said? "Ginger's eyes were closed," he snapped.

"What does that mean? You've not making sense."

"It means *after* Ginger fell someone was there and shut her eyes. It was no accident."

**Books by Lyn Cote**

Love Inspired Suspense

Love Inspired

*Sisters of the Heart

## LYN COTE

now lives in Wisconsin with her husband, her real-life hero. They raised a son and daughter together. Lyn has spent her adult life as a schoolteacher, a full-time mom and now a writer. Her favorite food is watermelon. Realizing that this delicacy is only available one season out of the year, Lyn's friends keep up a constant flow of watermelon gifts—candles, wood carvings, pillows, cloth bags, candy and on and on. Lyn also enjoys crocheting and knitting, watching *Wheel of Fortune* and doing lunch with friends. By the way, Lyn's last name is pronounced Coty.

Lyn enjoys hearing from readers, who can contact her at P.O. Box 864, Woodruff, WI 54568 or by e-mail at l.cote@juno.com.

# DANGEROUS SECRETS

## Lyn Cote

Steeple
Hill®

Published by Steeple Hill Books™

STEEPLE HILL BOOKS

Steeple
Hill®

ISBN-13: 978-0-373-44252-2
ISBN-10:    0-373-44252-1

DANGEROUS SECRETS

www.SteepleHill.com

**Printed in U.S.A.**

"Do not store up for yourselves treasures on earth, where moth and rust destroy, and where thieves break in and steal. But store up for yourselves treasures in heaven, where moth and rust do not destroy, and where thieves do not break in and steal."
—*Matthew* 6:18–20

"For the love of money is a root of all kinds of evil. Some people, eager for money, have wandered from the faith and pierced themselves with many griefs."
—*1 Timothy* 6:9–10

To Eunice, Ed and Jeanine,
thanks for a great summer!

# PROLOGUE

*March 1*

She'd managed to climb in a rear window, her heart pounding with fear and exertion. Had anyone seen her? At this time of night in this little burg? She doubted it. Standing in the apartment lit only by her flashlight and thin moonlight coming through the windows, she laid her flashlight on the floor. Where should she start looking? It had all seemed so easy when the idea had first come to her.

She approached a built-in bookcase. As she reached up to remove the books from the top shelf, it began. The wall in front of her eyes started to undulate as if an earthquake were taking place. Then the floor beneath her feet began to ripple. She staggered and caught hold of the bookcase, cursing.

And then she heard footsteps coming up the stairs. Or was that just part of the flashback, too?

# ONE

*March 2*

*Sylvie, I am going to wow you with a big surprise tomorrow!* What could Ginger's wow surprise be? This question kept bobbing to the surface of Sylvie Patterson's mind—interrupting her work. She sat at her PC near the front of her store, My Favorite Books, answering customer e-mails.

Last night Ginger, her favorite cousin, had blown into Winfield, intending to spend the next two months in her apartment above Sylvie's bookstore. Just a few years younger than Sylvie, Ginger would be busy "polishing" her dissertation on Alaskan whales. Last night Ginger, with her long, curly red hair and golden freckles, had been more effervescent than usual.

And in just a few more minutes, Sylvie would close up shop and find out what Ginger's big secret was.

The little bell on her shop's door jingled and cold

air swished inside. In the off-season, Sylvie didn't usually look up from her monitor to see who'd come in. But today it might be Ginger.

She glanced up. Not Ginger.

Ridge Matthews looked back at her. He stood there against the wall, which was lined with shelves and shelves of books.

Waves of recognition on so many different levels undulated through her. So much history lay between them. A tide of remembrance billowed in the conscious silence between her and Ridge. Ridge was still tall but not too tall, still broad-shouldered, and still possessed the same dark brown, nearly black, very serious eyes. Only a few glints of gray in his short-cropped hair reminded her that eighteen years had passed since he'd been a year-round resident of Winfield.

"Sylvie," he acknowledged her with the grave voice he'd acquired that awful summer night eighteen years ago.

"Ridge," she returned the greeting and forced a smile. She rose, holding out her hand. *I'm surprised to see you, Ridge, but not unhappy. Never unhappy.*

As if there were an invisible line etched in sand between them, he hesitated a split second and then came forward and gripped her hand—briefly.

He was still as buttoned-up as his black wool winter coat. Last December, she'd glimpsed him at a wedding, another of his rare visits. And now she thought she knew his reason for appearing here today. "Are you looking for Ben?" she asked. "He's running an errand for me."

Ridge digested this in several moments of silence. "My mother said he doesn't come home after school. Every day he walks here from the bus stop."

*Yes, going home to your parents' house is way too depressing for any kid.* For a long time, the Matthewses' home had been nothing but a house, merely four walls, a roof and floor. That was why Ridge had forsaken Winfield.

"Thanks for being kind to Ben." His low tone curled through her.

Resisting his effect on her, she forced another smile. "Ben's a good kid. Are you here to visit him for a few days?" she added, hoping his answer would be yes.

"I'm moving him away this weekend."

She stiffened with shock. "With you to Madison? Now?"

The door opened behind Ridge. More frigid air rushed in.

"No," Ridge said, "an opening has come up unexpectedly in a good military school near Milwaukee. Ben was next on the waiting list. He's scheduled to start bright and early on Monday."

Just inside her door, blond-haired and freckle-faced Ben halted, looking as if he'd just received the death sentence.

She took an involuntary step toward him. Military school? For Ben? *No.*

"Military school?" Ridge's orphaned ward echoed her aloud. "Monday?"

Sylvie wanted to pull Ben, now white-faced, into a protective hug. But at twelve, he was too old for that.

Caught between the two of them, Ridge shifted sideways, eyeing both. "Ben, you know I told you that my parents are too old to keep you."

Besides being too self-centered, too self-absorbed, Sylvie amended silently. The constant ache in her damaged hip twinged at this thought. *Ridge, don't be so cold. He's just a kid and he's been through so much.*

"I thought—" Ben's voice thinned "—you were going to get a place big enough for me to come live with you."

Ben's plaintive tone stung Sylvie.

Ridge had enough conscience to look uncomfortable. "My job doesn't make me good guardian material, Ben. I travel all over the state on homicide cases. Or I get embroiled in local ones that keep me out all hours of the day and night. This way you won't be shifted around from house to house while I'm tied up on a case. You'll be at school and I'll come and get you at least one weekend a month."

"What about this summer?" Ben asked, an edge of panic in his voice. "Sylvie said she'd teach me how to snorkel."

Ridge looked distinctly uneasy now. "I've signed you up for summer camp—"

"No!" Ben burst out.

"Ridge," Sylvie put in, overriding Ben's heated stream of objections, "my dad and I want Ben to spend the summer with us. I meant to ask you."

Silence.

"Really?" Ben asked, approaching her as if she were his last hope.

The spur-of-the-moment invitation had been forced out of her. She reached for Ben and he came to a halt beside her. She rested a hand on his shoulder. "Yes, and Milo planned to hire you to help him at the bait shop." Her father hadn't said so in so many words, but he liked kids in general and Ben in particular.

"Really?" Ben repeated, color coming back to his cheeks.

"Really." She squeezed Ben's shoulder and then glanced at Ridge, reading his chagrin, wanting to shake him, reach him. "You trust us with Ben, don't you, Ridge?" She knew this last phrase would make it impossible for him to say no. He wouldn't stir the murky waters of the past.

"Of course," he said brusquely. "Time for us to go, Ben." Peremptorily, he turned toward the door.

Again, some impishness prompted Sylvie to refuse to let Ridge have his way completely. Perhaps it was Ridge's aloof, almost insensitive handling of Ben that made her want to throw another speed bump in his path.

"Just a moment," she said. "Let me shut down my computer and we'll go upstairs. Ginger's back. She'll want to see you. Just got in last night."

"From Alaska?" Ridge asked, showing that he wasn't completely out of touch with Winfield.

"Yes, she plans to 'hole up' and finish her master's thesis. I haven't seen her at all today. She's probably still glued to her laptop upstairs in her apartment. I need to pry her loose. Then we'll go to pick up the pizza I ordered and then I'll take Ginger home with me to eat it." Sylvie bustled around turning off her computer.

Ben, who'd spent every afternoon after school with her since he'd moved in with the Matthewses last fall, went around turning off lights, helping her close up as usual.

Within minutes, Ridge and Ben stood near as she locked up, protecting her from the stiff wind. Ridge's presence made her feel everything more intensely—the cold, the wind, the early darkness. But without revealing this, she locked up the front door of the two-story Victorian that she rented from Ginger's mother. Once it was secured, the two males followed her limping gait. As they walked the narrow shoveled sidewalk around the side of the house, their footsteps crunched loudly in the clear early night.

The only other sound was the cutting wind blowing from Lake Superior at their backs. Sylvie tried to think of some way to hint to Ridge that she wanted to discuss Ben with him. But if the past was any guide, she knew Ridge would do anything to avoid being alone in her company.

The threesome reached the rear door of the enclosed two-story porch that shielded the back staircase. Sylvie unlocked and opened the door, ready to call up the stairs to her cousin. Then her heart stopped for one beat.

At the bottom of the steep staircase lay her cousin, crumpled. The deep winter dusk made Sylvie doubt her eyesight. She hurried over the threshold. "Ginger! Ginger!"

No response.

Sylvie threw herself onto her knees beside Ginger's body. No one alive would lie in that rigid, twisted position. Sylvie knew she must be dead. "Ginger!" she keened. "Ginger! No!"

Ridge heard the hysteria in Sylvie's voice. Taking the scene in at a glance, he recognized all the signs of death—death that had taken place hours before. He shoved Ben back out the door. "Go home. Now!"

"But…but," Ben sputtered.

"She's dead," Ridge hissed beside Ben's ear. "You need to go home and stay there."

"Sylvie—"

"I'll take care of her." Ridge pushed Ben farther away. "Go. I'll handle this. I'll take care of Sylvie. Go."

Looking fearfully over his shoulder, Ben fled, letting the outside door slam.

Ridge turned and knelt beside Sylvie. He went through the motions of checking Ginger Johnson's nonexistent pulse. He lifted her eyelids. Her irises were dilated. But…her eyes were closed. The thought made his insides congeal. Not just for the sorrow death always brought but because that meant…he didn't want to go there. For so many reasons.

He snapped open his cell phone and punched in the emergency number. He gave the details as simply as possible to the responder. He snapped it shut again. "Sylvie," he said gently, "help is on the way."

"She's dead, isn't she?" Rocking on her knees, Sylvie had wrapped her arms around herself as if she might fly apart.

"It looks like it." He didn't mention Ginger's eyes being closed. It hit him then. This was the second time he and Sylvie had together confronted the body of a relative, lying dead. He felt sick in the pit of his stomach. In spite of himself, he laid a hand on her slender shoulder.

She covered his hand with hers. "Ridge, Ginger must have fallen last night," she pleaded. "I think I would have heard her fall if…if it happened while

I was in the store." She looked up at him, her woebegone face pale and fringed by her short silvery-blond hair.

He read in her huge blue-violet eyes the silent plea for exoneration. Had this event taken her back in time, too, back to the night Dan had died? "Yes, you're right. From what I see I think Ginger must have fallen last night." *You didn't fail your cousin. She was dead before you came to work this morning.*

But he didn't let any of his suspicions about Ginger's fatal tumble color his tone or expression. If only Ginger's eyes had been open. How easy everything would have been.

With relief, he heard a police siren. Gently he grasped Sylvie by the upper arms and drew her to her feet. She felt unsteady to him. So one arm under hers, he guided her to the door. "I'm going to ask you to go back into your bookstore. Why don't you make a new pot of coffee?"

She looked up at him. Her lips were pressed so tightly together they were as white as the swirled frost on the single-pane window behind her. "I want my dad."

Another sting. She'd said those exact same words to him on that long-ago night, too. "Call Milo. He should be here. Ginger's mom, Shirley, still lives here year-round in her Victorian, right?"

She nodded. "But she and Tom are away in Arizona for a delayed honeymoon, a break before the tourist season starts in May." Tears filled her eyes. "I'll go…I'll go make the coffee."

After giving her a heartening squeeze, Ridge nudged her through the doorway. That was all she could do, all anyone could do now. Make coffee for the very long night ahead. He couldn't help himself; his gaze followed Sylvie's slender silhouette until she disappeared around the corner at the front.

The long night of investigating the crime scene had finally come to an end. Ridge glanced at his watch, his eyes gritty with fatigue. Nearly three o'clock in the early morning. Sheriff Keir Harding, whom Ridge remembered from high school, faced him at the bottom of the stairwell. Ginger's body had been taken away hours before.

"I don't think we can deny that Ginger's death is suspicious," Keir said. "But I don't want to start rumors."

"Having an autopsy done—people will hear about it and talk," Ridge said, rubbing his taut forehead. As they stood there talking, the coroner was probably wrapping up the autopsy at the local funeral home.

Keir grimaced. "Ginger was well liked. This will hit everyone hard."

*I couldn't agree with you more.*

"Let's send Sylvie and her dad home, then." Keir led Ridge to the door he'd entered hours ago with

Sylvie and Ben. "We'll lock this place up tight and I'll make sure a deputy checks around here every hour so the crime scene isn't tampered with." The sheriff made a sound of exhaustion.

Outside in the silence of the stark, icy night, they walked single file on the path between the waist-high mounds of snow around to the front. Sylvie's bookstore was still alight on the quiet street of darkened shops and homes.

"I'm so glad you were already in town. This saves me calling for state help." After delivering these unwelcome words, Keir bid him good-night and headed for his sheriff's Jeep.

Ridge fumed in silence, but his fatigue even dulled this reaction. This was supposed to be just a quick trip home to take care of settling Ben. But Ginger hadn't gotten herself killed just to trouble him. *My problems are nothing compared to Ginger's family's.*

Now he had to face Sylvie. Ridge stiffened his defenses and walked into the entrance of the bookshop. Visibly despondent, Sylvie was draped over a well-worn tweedy sofa along the wall in the foyer. She glanced up at him, her appealing face drawn.

"Where's Milo?" he asked, forestalling her questions.

She sat up. "Dad went home hours ago to call his sister, Shirley, and break the news to her about

Ginger. He also wanted to make flight arrangements for her and Tom on his computer while they packed to come home."

He watched her slip her small feet back into her stylish black boots. "Rough."

Their eyes connected. And he sensed that everything that he wished to conceal from her about Ginger's death and about everything else that lay between him and Sylvie, she read with ease. His jaw clenched. He tried to relax it. And failed.

A tear trickled down Sylvie's right cheek. She brushed it away and stood. "I take it I can go home now."

Ridge nodded, unable to speak. Images from the scene of Dan's untimely death had slid in and out of his conscious thoughts during the night-long investigation. Bringing Sylvie along with them.

She went to the coatrack and Ridge hurried forward to help her don her plum-colored down coat the second time tonight. In her evident fatigue, she wavered on her feet. He steadied her, a hand on her upper arm.

"I'm fine," she whispered.

Her frailty belied her words. He admired her nerve. Nothing was fine tonight and nothing would be fine for quite a while. "My car's out front."

He escorted her through turning off the foyer lights, locking up, and then out in the winter cold so dry the air almost crackled with static electricity. After helping her into his SUV, he got in and turned the key in the ignition. Nothing. He tried again. Not even grinding. Sudden aggravation flamed through him. With his gloved palm, he slapped the steering wheel once. Nothing ever went right for him in Winfield.

"You left your lights on," Sylvie said, pointing to the dash where sure enough his lights had been switched on and left.

He let out a slow breath. "I'm used to the automatic ones but I must have turned them on manually and forgot."

"And when you arrived, the street was still lit by shop lights along with the streetlamps. You wouldn't have noticed you'd left them on. No one did." She opened her door. "It's only a few blocks for me. I always walk to work. And your parents' house is within walking distance. Leave it till morning."

Not willing to let her out of his sight, he got out and joined her on the sidewalk. The icy temperature nearly took his breath away. It was probably quite safe for her to walk home, but after finding Ginger dead, he didn't want to leave Sylvie alone at the dark early-morning hour. He would only leave her when she was in her own home safe with her father. "I'll walk you home first."

"That's not necessary. This is Winfield, remember?" She stopped speaking—abruptly.

Her face was turned away from the streetlamp so

he couldn't see her expression, but her sudden silence and immobility told him that Ginger's death had hit her afresh. Yes, this was Winfield, but Ginger had died, not in faraway Alaska, but here in her hometown of Winfield.

Without mentioning this, he looped Sylvie's arm around the crook of his and began leading her down the street he knew so well. He didn't need to ask her where her house was. Walking beside Sylvie made him very sensitive to the stark white of the snow mounds left by the plows. It also made him aware that the cold, along with being in Winfield, was nibbling away at him bit by bit.

After a couple of steps, he adjusted to accommodate her halting gait. This nipped his conscience. He'd been able to walk away from Dan's accident unscathed. But did every limping step remind Sylvie of the past? If it did, how did she stand it?

"What took the sheriff so long?" she asked. "I mean, why did they spend so much time up in her apartment?"

Uneasiness twitched through him. He didn't want to face this. No, he did not. They reached the end of the block and started up the next. How to avoid making this damaging revelation?

"Ridge?" she prompted.

"Sylvie, it's late. We can talk about this tomorrow."

Sylvie halted. "You're frightening me. What aren't you telling me?"

"Come along." He tugged her.

She resisted. "I'm not moving until you tell me why they took so long up in Ginger's apartment."

He'd had it. Why didn't anything ever go the easy way? Why couldn't she just accept what he said? "Ginger's death has been deemed suspicious."

"Suspicious?"

The low temp was numbing his bare ears. "It's freezing out. Don't you feel it?" He tugged her elbow. "Come on. I'll tell you everything. Let's just get out of this cold." He drew her along.

"Tell me," she insisted, even though she began walking again.

He walked faster, urging her along. "Ginger's apartment had been ransacked."

"What? You mean someone broke in?" She slowed, pulling against him.

He tugged her. "Someone tore Ginger's apartment apart." His voice turned savage. *I wanted to leave in the morning. What's the chance of that now?* "We think the point of entry was a rear window on the back porch."

"What could they have been looking for?" she asked. "Ginger didn't have anything worth stealing."

That only made it more suspicious. Didn't Sylvie see that?

"Maybe you've got it wrong," Sylvie said. "Ginger might have been looking for something and had everything turned upside down and inside out. Ginger wasn't always very neat."

Ridge didn't want to respond to this excuse. Why not let her come up with ways to avoid the truth? He just slogged on, the relentless cold filtering through all his layers of clothing.

"Don't you think it could be that? Ginger might just have been unpacking and—"

The sheriff's words came back to Ridge: "It's good you were with Sylvie when she found the body. She might have closed her cousin's eyes without thinking or I might have assumed that she did. But we both know—" Suddenly Ridge had had it. He couldn't take any more waffling, any more lame explanations. "Ginger's eyes were closed," he snapped.

"What does that mean?" Sylvie halted again. "You're not making sense."

He urged her along again. His face was stiff not just from the bitter temperature but now from irritation. "It means that someone closed her eyes."

"Someone…what?"

His patience evaporated. "Sylvie, if a person falls to their death, their eyes will remain open. Someone was there *after* Ginger fell and shut her eyes."

Sylvie exhaled—deeply and loudly. And then began breathing very fast.

In the scant light from the streetlamp, he glimpsed her eyes and mouth wide in shock. Then he realized she wasn't getting her breath. "Sylvie." He shook her arms. "Sylvie."

She was beginning to hyperventilate. If he didn't get her breathing, she'd faint on him.

He pulled her face close to his and, covering her mouth with his, blew into her open mouth. Once. Twice. He shook her again. On and on, he blew carbon dioxide into her mouth. "Breathe. Breathe."

She shuddered once and pulled away from his mouth. Then she leaned her head against him. She was gasping now, but was getting air. "This," she whispered, "can't be happening."

Not wanting to, but unable to stop himself, he put his arms around her delicate form. "It's freezing. I've got to get you home."

She raised her pale face to him, visible now in the streetlamp glow. "What happens now?"

# TWO

*March 5, Saturday afternoon*

Sylvie's insides were descending, spiraling as if she were going down a narrow funnel. For the hundredth time, she pulled herself up from the darkness that was trying to suck her under. Surviving Ginger's funeral had devoured all her strength. But she was determined to be a support to her family.

The bright fluorescent lighting in the church basement hurt her eyes. She hadn't slept very much over the past three nights. But neither had anyone else in her family. Now, she sat at a long white-paper-covered table near the end of the after-funeral luncheon. In the cement-block basement room, the men all wore dark suits. The women had dressed in sober dresses or dark pantsuits. The dark colors matched the mood in the room. Unexpressed grief revealed itself in the tight smiles and lowered voices. Rhinestone brooches on collars glinted here and there in the bright light. Almost everyone in town had turned out for the funeral. Cousins and relations murmured to each other down the length of the family table. Subdued, guarded. This death was different. This was unnatural. Perhaps murder.

Her father sat across from her next to his new brother-in-law, Tom Robson, while her aunt Shirley, Ginger's mother, sat beside Sylvie. Neither of them spoke though occasionally her aunt forced a smile for her and patted her arm as if trying to make up for the horrible fact that Sylvie had been the one to find Ginger. Shirley's sorrow appeared still too deep for tears.

"I hope Chad didn't have trouble finding it," Ginger's stepfather, Tom, fretted, glancing at the large wall clock.

In the distracted haze they were all in today, Tom had forgotten to bring his wallet and he wanted to give Pastor Ray the check he'd already written him for doing the funeral service. Chad, Shirley's teenage foster son, had gone to fetch it.

The gathering was about to break up. The forced-air furnace was having trouble keeping away the encroaching chill that penetrated the basement room. Small children were starting to whimper and whine, rubbing their eyes as it neared time for their afternoon naps. And the church women who'd put on the luncheon were in the kitchen, chatting, clattering, washing casserole dishes and coffee cups. The homey sounds comforted Sylvie. Here she was surrounded by friends and family. It was at times like these that the ties of blood and faith meant the most.

Sylvie surreptitiously massaged her sore hip. She'd played the organ for the funeral and then done a lot of walking through snow and standing at the interment. Her hip had no cartilage to keep bone from rubbing on bone. At home tonight she'd have to use an ice pack on her hip to bring down the swelling.

Aunt Shirley lowered her voice and spoke into Sylvie's ear, asking about another cousin. "Rae-Jean's still coming home on Monday?"

Sylvie nodded. Rae-Jean had just finished a term at the Chippewa Drug Treatment Facility and a few months in prison. "Dad's going to drive down to get her."

"Her parents still haven't forgiven her?" Aunt Shirley asked.

Sylvie shook her head.

Aunt Shirley lowered her chin, frowning. She didn't have to say the words. Sylvie understood the unspoken message. Rae-Jean's parents should be grateful that they still had their daughter alive and breathing. No matter what she'd done.

Sylvie watched Tom fidget, glancing at the clock again. What was taking Chad so long to get back? Tom and Shirley's house wasn't that far away. Sylvie felt her patience dissolving, fizzing away like a cold tablet in water. *Come on, Chad. We can't leave till you bring the check.*

Once again, flashes, images from the evening when she'd found Ginger ricocheted in her mind. Ridge hadn't come today. Nor his parents. Which had been the usual for them. And no one could blame them. Ridge had been busy most of every day working with the sheriff, sifting the evidence collected at Ginger's apartment. Audra Harding had represented her husband, the sheriff, and was in the kitchen washing dishes.

Sylvie couldn't get Ridge out of her mind. They'd been so close the night he'd walked her home. For just those few dark moments, the past hadn't weighed them down. She'd needed comfort and he'd offered it. She could still feel his warm breath reviving her, his strong chest under his woolen coat supporting her. For that instant, he'd let her come close, so close.

Wild-eyed, Chad appeared at the bottom of the stairwell and stood gasping as if he'd run all the way.

Sitting at his parents' kitchen table, Ridge tried to get a word into the phone conversation. But his boss, Matt Block, in Madison hadn't finished with him yet. "Harding has a good rep. He's had a couple of tricky cases that he solved since he took over as sheriff."

Ridge was aware of this but he couldn't butt in and say so. One didn't do that with Block. Ridge heard himself grinding his molars to keep from interrupting his boss.

"Don't hurry back," Block continued, "until Harding thinks he can handle it on his own. Let him decide."

While listening to Block fill him in on what was going on in Madison, Ridge moved the salt and pepper shakers closer together and glanced at his watch. The funeral luncheon should be winding up about now. His ward, Ben sat, staring at him from the opposite end of the table. Didn't the kid ever blink?

Block repeated that he wanted Ridge to stay in Winfield. Ridge forced himself to speak in an even tone. "That might take some time."

"Like I said, nothing pressing here now," Block said, infuriating Ridge further. "And we want to keep our funding at the same level for the next fiscal year. Every time our people go out to work with local law enforcement, it's good PR. This close to the state house we've got to think of politics, next year's budget. Keep me posted." And Block hung up.

For a moment, Ridge wanted to toss the cordless receiver into the garbage disposal. And grind it to dust. *I don't want to stay here.*

"What did your boss say?" Ben asked.

Ridge made himself look the kid in the eye. It wasn't the kid's fault that he had his mom's blue eyes and his dad's cowlicky hairline. "I'll be staying for a while longer."

Ben's pleased reaction was not obvious, but of course, the kid still made it clear he didn't want to leave Winfield.

From the next room, the musical theme from a soap opera his mother was watching blared louder, no doubt time for another string of commercials. And though practically every other year-round resident in Winfield was in the community church basement for Ginger's funeral, his dad was at his grocery store as he was seven days a week every week. Didn't his parents ever look beyond the caves they'd retreated into?

*I can't take this all out on Ben.* But on the way to Winfield just a few days ago, Ridge had felt so confident that everything was working out so well for his getting the kid settled. The opening at the military school, the camp registration. Now all this.

The phone rang. Ridge picked up. What he heard made him rise to his feet.

Ben rose, too, watchful.

Ridge hung up and hurried to the row of wooden pegs by the back door where all the coats hung. Ben rushed up behind him and grabbed his jacket, too.

Ridge stopped and faced Ben. "I'm going out on police business. Stay here."

Ben shoved ahead of Ridge to the back door. "I'm not staying here." The kid burst outside and ran down the shoveled sidewalk to Ridge's SUV. There he grabbed the door handle.

"This is police business," Ridge barked. "No place for a kid. You can't come with me."

"Then drop me at the church where everybody is. I can hang with Milo or a friend. I'll walk home for supper."

Ridge had thought Ben going to a funeral so soon after losing his parents would be bad for him. But he couldn't blame the kid for wanting to get out of his parents' house. After all, it was exactly what he wanted to do. "Okay. I'll drop you at the church. Get in." Ridge got into the car.

"What happened?" Ben said inside, hooking his seat belt.

"I can't tell you until the sheriff wants it known."

After dropping Ben at the church, Ridge drove the few blocks to Tom and Shirley's house. He still couldn't believe what the sheriff's dispatch had told him.

Two sheriff's vehicles were already parked outside the white Victorian. Ridge strode up the freshly shoveled walk to the front door. It opened before he could knock. Keir Harding waited for him just inside. He looked disgruntled and Ridge didn't blame him. He was disgruntled, too.

"Who notified you?" Ridge asked, looking around at the disarray inside the house.

"Shirley's foster son, Chad. He came alone to pick up Tom's wallet. Tom had forgotten it this morning. Chad found the door open. He looked inside, couldn't believe what he saw and froze up. Finally he ran back to the church and announced what had happened to the general public."

*Great. Nothing like a little discretion.* "What do you think? Just an opportunist taking advantage of the funeral?"

"Here in Winfield?" Keir nearly snarled. "This isn't Madison or Milwaukee. Most of the town is at the funeral. Tom and Shirley, not to mention Ginger, are very well liked. If someone from Winfield did this, I'll swallow my badge."

Deputy Trish Lawson walked into the room. Wearing thin plastic gloves, she held up a man's wallet.

"Where did you find it?" Keir asked.

"On the top of the bedroom dresser. In plain sight." Trish's mouth flattened into a grim line. "It hasn't been touched." She opened the wallet to show them the credit cards and greenbacks still inside.

Ridge processed what had just been revealed. Someone had broken into Shirley's Victorian. But they hadn't bothered to swipe the wallet sitting out or even take the money out of it. He looked at the sheriff. They didn't need to say it aloud. Both of them wanted to know—what's going on here?

Later that day, Ridge had tried to beg off from going to Milo's place to fill in Ginger's family about this latest development in the case. Neither

Ridge nor Keir had even bothered to discuss the possibility that the two break-ins might not be related. Of course they were. And Keir wanted Ridge along. After all, this was what Ridge, a state homicide detective, was being paid to do by the state of Wisconsin.

Now they entered the protected stairwell at the side of Milo's Bait and Tackle on the waterfront and walked up the one steep flight of stairs to the apartment above the store. The door opened before the sheriff could knock.

Still wearing her dark violet pantsuit, Sylvie stood at the door. Her white-gold hair shimmered in the light. "We heard your footsteps." She stepped back, allowing the sheriff and Ridge into the kitchen, which opened onto the large front room. Around the crowded table sat Milo, Ginger's parents, Chad and Ben, who avoided Ridge's gaze. Ridge looked away, too. Ginger's mother, Shirley, and her new husband, Tom, were in so much emotional pain that their faces actually looked pasty gray.

Keir cleared his throat. "We've gone over your place thoroughly."

"What was taken?" Milo asked.

"Nothing obvious." Keir held out Tom's wallet and Ridge set the small wooden jewelry box on the table in front of Shirley. "Both of you," the sheriff continued, "please check these out and tell me if you are missing anything."

Tom stared at the wallet and then opened it. He pulled out the pastor's check and then counted the bills. At the same time, Shirley opened and closed all the tiny drawers in the jewelry box. Both of them looked up at the same time. "Nothing's missing," Tom said.

"Same here," Shirley agreed.

Ridge felt like throwing something fragile at the wall just to hear the sound of something, anything, breaking. None of this made the least bit of sense, but all of it was keeping him just where he didn't want to be. Wait until his boss heard this development. He'd insist Ridge stay put. And to make matters worse, he found himself glancing once again toward Sylvie's cap of shining hair.

"Let's drive you to the house, then," Keir said, "and you can look around and tell us if anything is missing."

"But we didn't leave valuables at home when we left for our winter break," Shirley objected. "We have a safety-deposit box in a bank in Ashford. If they didn't take Tom's wallet or my few pieces of Black Hills Gold, there isn't anything of value in the house."

"Are you sure?" Ridge asked, hoping they'd recall something. Wintry wind gusted against the large front windows overlooking the waterfront.

"We lost nothing of value," Tom said with finality. "Winfield doesn't have much crime, but we didn't want to leave any temptation for anyone—"

"That's right," Shirley agreed again, "especially after everything that happened to Rae-Jean last year."

The two of them couldn't have said anything that Ridge wanted less to hear. *How am I going to get Ben to that school by Sunday, by tomorrow night?* Outside the windows, the implacable frozen expanse of the shore of Lake Superior stretched far north on the horizon.

"This couldn't have anything to do with Rae-Jean coming home this week, could it?" Milo asked.

"I don't see how," the sheriff responded. "Her supplier is in prison for a nice long sentence for dealing. And he's not the kind of person anyone would miss. At least, that's my take on it. Did Rae-Jean ever stop by your place last year?"

"No," Tom said.

"So the idea that someone might be looking for a stash of drugs at our place is foolish," Shirley said, seconding her husband.

"Well, sometimes drug users do really stupid things," Keir said. "Let's go. I want you to walk through the house with me just in case you can pinpoint what someone took or might have been looking for. It might be something without obvious value to me."

Tom and Shirley, with Milo along for moral support, left with Keir. Ben stayed at the table. Sylvie closed the door behind them against the icy wind winnowing up the stairwell. Ridge stared across the kitchen at Sylvie. In spite of himself.

Sylvie felt a sudden relief when Tom and Shirley left. She'd been holding it together for their sake. Now she sank down at the table and bent her head in her hand. Tears slid down her cheeks. Still mindful of Ben and Ridge, she wept quietly so as not to upset either male with out-of-control sobbing. She was very aware that Ridge had been keeping his eyes on her since he entered. "I'm sorry," she whispered. "It's been a very rough day." *And it might become rougher. What does Ridge think is going on here?*

Ben tentatively patted her shoulder. "I'm sorry your cousin died."

Sylvie caught his hand and squeezed it. "Thanks, Ben." Remembering his recent loss, she smiled tremulously at him. "I'll be fine. I just wish this all hadn't happened. Why don't you go turn the TV on? It's time for that show you like on Animal Planet."

Ben looked relieved and left the room. Soon they heard the noise of the TV.

She looked up at Ridge. "What's going on here?" she asked in a low voice so Ben wouldn't hear.

Ridge sat down as if suddenly drained of energy. "It's all screwy. We can discover no motive at all for Ginger's death. We don't even know if her death was somehow accidental or premeditated murder."

"What does that mean?" Sylvie asked, watching

the way his strong hands folded into fists. *This isn't your fault, Ridge.*

"She might have surprised someone going through the apartment and they might have hit her or knocked her down the stairs."

"But what could anybody be looking for?" Sylvie asked, not bothering to ask why they would accidentally kill Ginger and then shut her eyes. None of this made any sense. "My aunt and uncle and Ginger aren't wealthy or into drugs. So what else is there to find in their homes?"

Ridge made a sound of disgust. "Well, that's the crux of the problem, isn't it? What is there to commit murder for in Ginger's apartment?"

Ridge always cared so much. He'd been away for years yet Ginger's death was obviously infuriating him.

"I've been thinking and thinking. The only thing that I keep coming back to is that when I left her that night—" Sylvie strengthened her self-control, tightening her quivering lips "—Ginger said she was going to have a wow surprise for me in the morning."

"She did?" Ridge shook his head and leaned forward. "What do you think she meant?"

"I asked her if it was going to be an engagement ring." She studied his hands, so powerful-looking with blunt fingertips. Who had done this and unknowingly taken on this formidable man as an adversary?

"A ring? From whom?"

"I knew she'd been dating a young assistant professor in Alaska." Sylvie sighed. Her conversation with Ginger just three days before felt like a million years ago. "But when I guessed that he'd popped the question, Ginger only giggled and said that I'd see tomorrow. Her surprise was going to knock my socks out of the park." Sylvie couldn't help half smiling over Ginger's playing with words. That had been part of her.

"We didn't find an engagement ring among Ginger's belongings," Ridge said. "And I don't see anyone ransacking an apartment for an engagement ring that an assistant professor could afford."

"And he didn't come to the funeral," Sylvie added, feeling doors slamming inside her, closing out her cousin's young life. "The very next day after we found…after Ginger's death, I called her professor, the one who was overseeing her research, and told him to pass the news around that Ginger had…had died. They sent flowers, but—" Sylvie lifted her eyes to Ridge's dark somber ones "—the assistant prof didn't show up here. If he'd proposed he would have come, wouldn't he?"

"You would think so." Ridge's usually business-like face twisted with evident dissatisfaction and he switched topics. "Tomorrow is Sunday. I'm going to take the day off and drive Ben south to his school."

"No," Sylvie objected before she could stop herself. "Ridge, I really think that military school for Ben right now is ill-advised. I know you didn't ask my opinion, but this just doesn't feel right." Impetuously she reached over and laid her hand on his arm. Trying to sway him somehow.

He turned away and her hand fell. "Sylvie, I don't know why Ben's parents put me down as Ben's guardian. They never asked me and if they had, I would have suggested they choose someone else. My lifestyle—"

Sylvie didn't know Ben's parents. Ben's father and mother had been college friends of Ridge's who had died in a boating accident the year before in Green Bay. "Then leave Ben here. Maybe he can do some good. Maybe his presence will goad your parents into starting to live again." She hadn't meant to say that. She looked down, not wanting to meet Ridge's gaze. "Sorry," she whispered.

"To shake my parents out of their apathy, it would take something more on the order of an atomic bomb." Ridge's voice was bitter. "I know you mean it out of goodness, Sylvie. But even after eighteen years, my parents are still just breathing, just existing. Ben has been with them for months. Do you honestly see any change?"

She couldn't lie. "No. None."

"They don't want him in their house. They ignore the kid. If they can help it, they don't even look at him. That can't be good for him."

Suddenly chilled, Sylvie folded her arms around

herself. Maybe they didn't want Ben because he was the same age as Dan had been when he died.

"Hey—" Ridge touched her shoulder but briefly "—this isn't your fault. Thanks for befriending Ben. And I'll consider letting Ben come to spend a few weeks in the summer with you. If you still want him."

"I do." She looked up into Ridge's dark, dark eyes, seeing the regret, the uneasiness there. She smoothed her hand over her shoulder where he'd touched her.

"And don't worry about Ben," Ridge said gruffly. "He'll be safe, well fed and they have a counselor on staff and he knows that Ben recently lost his parents. It's really a good place for Ben to be right now."

She nodded, unconvinced. But Ridge was Ben's guardian. She wasn't. *I'm turning this over to You, God. If You have a better plan for Ben, You'll have to put it into motion. I can't do anything.* And on top of everything else, she had Rae-Jean coming home on Monday.

*March 6, Sunday*

In the crisp morning light, Ridge raced up the steps to Milo and Sylvie's apartment. He pounded on the door. His pulse throbbed at his temples.

Sylvie opened it, dressed in her Sunday best. "Ridge, what's wrong—"

"Is Ben here?"

"Here? What's happened?" she asked, stepping back.

Ridge came inside, shutting the door against the cold wind. "I got up to drive Ben to the military school and he wasn't in his bed."

She goggled at him. "What?"

"He's run away. Did he come here?"

"Of course not," Milo answered from the table where he sat with coffee and hot oatmeal. "We'd have called your parents' house if he'd shown up here."

"What about Sylvie's store? Does he know how to get in there?"

"He knows where I keep an extra key behind a loose piece of siding to the right of the door," Sylvie admitted.

Ridge turned immediately and headed out and down the steps.

"We'll be at church if you need us," Milo called after him.

Ridge didn't bother to reply. *This was all I needed.*

# THREE

*March 7*

Monday evening after work, Sylvie and her dad, Milo, reluctantly climbed up the steps to Ginger's apartment over Sylvie's store. The sheriff had said that he was done with this crime scene. Shirley and Tom were still dealing with too much—the loss of Ginger and the aftermath of the break-in at their house. So Sylvie and her father wanted to save Ginger's parents the burden of cleaning up the mess and packing up their daughter's things and putting them away. But Sylvie's mind kept going back to Ben. Had he run away yesterday? Or had someone taken him away?

The studio apartment was in shambles, books on the floor and Ginger's possessions strewn over the hardwood floor. "What should we do first?" It was all too much. She swallowed down her worry and sorrow, but the effort cost her. She felt like a rag doll minus her stuffing.

"Ginger didn't have time to eat anything, did she?" Milo asked.

"I don't think so. But I know right before we took off that evening, she dropped off a small plastic bag of groceries she'd picked up." Sylvie's throat tightened and she couldn't say more. Just thinking about the last fun evening with Ginger was like shards of glass penetrating her heart.

"Sweetheart, why don't you check the kitchen to see if anything needs washing up? I'll start cleaning in here." Her father's voice lacked its usual exuberance.

Sylvie wandered into the small alcove kitchen and glanced around. Nothing was on the counter or in the sink. She opened the refrigerator. Inside, a plastic half gallon of milk was a third full. And a peanut butter jar's lid was cockeyed. She lifted the jar and unscrewed the top. A generous dollop had been dug out and evidently eaten. A jar of strawberry jam had been similarly treated. A loaf of bread had been opened and not closed tightly.

She stared at the peanut butter jar in her hand, its nutty scent strong. That last night of her life, had Ginger had time to make and eat a peanut butter sandwich? Especially after all the Chinese food they'd consumed that evening? In view of

Ginger's love affair with peanut butter and straw-berry jam—perhaps.

Sylvie's mind felt mired, sluggish. Suddenly she didn't have any strength in her legs. She sat down at the tiny table beside the kitchen window and buried her head in her hands. *Ginger, I can't believe you're gone.*

Sylvie lost track of time. Finally, she realized that her father was speaking to her. She looked up.

"Sylvie, what's wrong?" Her dad made a face. "I mean besides the obvious."

Her lower lip trembled as she held out the peanut butter jar. Maybe it was just her grief, but the small inconsistency had unnerved her.

Milo frowned and took the jar from her. "What's the matter?"

"Did Ridge say anything about Ginger eating peanut butter that night?" she replied, making her voice stronger. "I mean, did she make herself a sandwich and then someone surprised her? Did the deputies help themselves to her food? I wouldn't think so, but…" *Ginger, oh, Ginger, who did this to you? Why?* "I…this just doesn't make any sense." She rested her head in her hand.

"I'll call the sheriff." Milo did just that. Then, closing his cell phone, he sat down across from her. "He says Ginger had eaten but he couldn't remember if peanut butter had been found in…" Her father's voice faltered. "Anyway, he saw the milk and bread in the fridge but it hadn't been touched. After dusting the containers for fingerprints, they left everything undisturbed."

"Did he say anything about the search for Ben?" She had to say the words though she knew Keir would have called *them* had there been any news.

Her dad shook his head.

"This doesn't make any sense." She covered her face with her shaky hands. "I just can't think tonight." Where would Ben have run to? "Let's get this over with, Dad." She heaved herself to her feet.

All the tragedy, all the mystery seemed to be chipping away at reality. She felt thinner, less substantial than the night she'd welcomed Ginger home. She drifted back into the main room of the small apartment which her father had put back in order. He followed her and then halted, his hands at his hips. "There wasn't much to put back into her suitcases. She hadn't really unpacked."

"Last fall she left stuff in her closet, I think," Sylvie muttered. "I mean, summer clothes and things she didn't need in Alaska."

"I don't think we need to dig into that yet. Let's just shove her luggage and stuff up into the attic. No one's going to want to rent this apartment for a long time. When a suspicious death takes place somewhere, people get spooked. They shouldn't, of course, but superstition still holds power over some."

He was right, of course. But perhaps summer

people who hadn't known Ginger wouldn't care. Milo and she worked together silently packing up the final few things that Ginger had pulled from her suitcases—before falling or being pushed to her death. That her brilliant cousin should be dead so tragically young reminded Sylvie of the research Ginger had spent the past winters collecting.

Enmeshed in the web of grief and worry, Sylvie looked around for Ginger's laptop with its smooth black nylon case. It contained all her files. Sylvie had seen it in Ginger's car that night Ginger and she had gone out. "Where's Ginger's laptop? I want to contact her professor. Perhaps someone can use Ginger's research for their thesis or dissertation. Ginger would hate to have all her work go to waste." She gazed around at the suitcases and duffels. In vain.

"Did we mention that to the sheriff?" her father asked. "Everything was such a shock—I didn't even think about her laptop."

"I didn't, either. But maybe they took it away as evidence." Sylvie went around the room, looking underneath furniture and behind doors and in the one closet. But of course neither the sheriff nor Ginger would put the laptop under a piece of furniture. Her brain must be unraveling. "Do you think that Keir did take it with him?"

Her father pulled out his cell phone and called Keir at home. "Sorry to bother you again, Keir," her father started his question. After a brief conversation, Milo looked at her. "He said they did not find a laptop, which Shirley had reported as missing. Not in her apartment nor in her car. I told him we would check the attic again. Then he told us to lock up tight and go home. He'll come and look everything over one more time tomorrow morning."

Her father reached up and pulled down the attic hatch and an accordion flight of narrow steps unfolded.

Someone above exclaimed in surprise.

Sylvie and her dad exchanged glances. With sudden relief, they knew who had been eating Ginger's food. "Ben!" her father shouted up. "Come down the steps, please."

Within moments Ben's worried face looked down at them in the low light.

"Ben," her dad said, his voice softening, "come down and help us put Ginger's stuff up in the attic. Then we'll talk."

Ridge sat at his parents' kitchen table alone. Since the soap operas were over for the day, his mother had already gone to bed. His dad was watching some sports event from somewhere in the world brought to him on the cable TV. The British voice of the broadcaster and distant fans cheering contrasted with Ridge's solitary vigil, awaiting news of Ben.

Ridge was tired, bone tired. He'd driven all over town and most of the county yesterday and today.

He'd called Ben's teacher here and she'd helped him contact all the students from Ben's class at school. None of them had seen or heard from Ben since school on Friday afternoon.

Ridge was sure that Ben had run away, not been grabbed. But where would he run to? Why hadn't he guessed that the boy might do that? *Why am I surprised? Nothing ever goes right when I come back to Winfield.*

Images of Ginger, Sylvie and his brother, Dan, at the same age as Ben flitted across the screen of his mind. The three were not connected in reality, but were tangled in the twisted knot of his dissatisfaction and loss.

He rose and poured himself another cup of the strong coffee from the percolator. It nearly burned his tongue, so he blew over the dark surface. He'd called the military school and left a message on their answering machine that Ben might not be able to come to school until Tuesday. What if they wouldn't wait? What if they gave the opening to the next kid on the list?

He sipped the bitter brew. His mind tried to take him back to Ben's mother and father. How had it happened that his two best friends could end up causing him such pain? Ridge resisted. No more unproductive trips down memory lane.

*All I've done, it seems, since I came to Winfield is give people bad news. I didn't think Ben would hate the idea of military school. Why didn't I realize he might become attached here? The answer to that is easy. I thought he'd be happy to get away from my parents' house.*

The phone rang. He picked up. The words he heard did not make him happy. But at least one mystery was solved.

He didn't bother to tell his dad that he was leaving. He merely put down the coffee mug and pulled on his winter coat. He hurried out to his SUV.

Sylvie opened the door and let Ridge into her apartment above her dad's bait shop. His face revealed a mixture of strain and frustration. She touched his arm, asking him silently to pause, to moderate his anger.

His eyes connected with hers and a hint of chagrin shaded his. But he didn't pull away from her touch.

She tightened her grip, aware of the latent strength in him. "Ben is very upset," she whispered, "please be kind."

Ridge grimaced. "I know he's had a rough time," he muttered, "but I need to get him established somewhere permanent, away from my parents. He will do better that way."

There was much that Sylvie could say to this. But she merely gestured him inside. She hung up his coat on one of the pegs by the door. They turned to the table where her dad and Ben sat, waiting.

"I don't want to go to that school," Ben insisted, his face flushed.

Ridge waited until Sylvie also sat down at the table and then he eased down, facing Ben. "I know you're afraid of going to a new school again—"

"I'm not afraid," Ben objected. "I just like it here." He glanced at Milo. "I don't want to leave Winfield."

Sylvie sat praying for God to open Ridge's mind and heart. Even when he was upset and she was in disagreement with him, he drew her to himself, compelled her to notice him. Long to be nearer to him. It would have been easier on her if he'd left with Ben as planned.

"Ben, you haven't even seen the school," Ridge coaxed. "It's really a good place. I'm just trying to get you settled somewhere…." He paused. "We're all tired and it's past your bedtime, Ben. Let's go home, okay?"

Sylvie appreciated Ridge's attempt to reassure Ben and she knew from his perspective that he was trying to do what was best for Ben. But he was wrong.

Ben bolted from the room. Milo rose and followed him.

Ridge had started to rise, but Sylvie pressed her hand on Ridge's forearm to stop him from following her dad. This time her touch connected her to him in a new way. Vibrations of both his strength and his vulnerability flowed from him up her arm.

"Ridge, let my dad talk to him."

"Ben is not your responsibility." He slipped away from her touch. "He's mine. But I don't seem to know how to connect with him. I only want to see him settled and doing well. There's just too much uncertainty in my lifestyle. He needs stability."

She let her hand fall; their vibrant connection severed. Why did he always pull away from her? She nearly asked him, "Why did Ben's parents choose you as Ben's guardian?" But she held the words in. Ridge was a good man, but he had no experience as a father. And he had lost his own family for all intents and purposes. Sylvie watched Ridge struggle with this letdown, this failure of his carefully laid plans. She lowered her gaze, not knowing what to say to make him understand Ben.

Then she recalled what she'd told the sheriff. "Ridge, Ginger's laptop was missing. Did Shirley mention that to you?"

"Yes, we're looking for it."

Milo returned to the kitchen. "Ridge," he said in a very low tone, "I left Ben working on tying fishing flies. I wanted to ask you something. If we could find a place for Ben here, could he stay in Winfield until the end of the summer?"

Ridge's expression stiffened. "Ben's my responsibility."

From under her half-closed eyes, Sylvie discerned offended pride as it flickered over Ridge's distinctive features.

"Ridge, it's hard for a kid to change schools in the middle of a year. Why not let Ben finish out the year here? I think I may have a solution."

"What are you thinking?" Ridge asked.

"Why not let Rae-Jean go to Shirley?" Milo asked. "And Ben comes here."

"At a sad time like this?" Ridge sounded uncertain.

"Having someone to take care of would help Shirley. I know my sister."

Ridge shrugged. "Okay. Ask."

Milo lifted the receiver of the kitchen wall phone and dialed a number. "I'm sorry to bother you so late, Tom."

Sylvie listened to the brief conversation, carried on in a low voice Ben couldn't overhear. And every word her father spoke made her love him more than she already did.

He hung up the phone. "Tom and Shirley will keep Rae-Jean with them. Ridge, we have room for Ben now. May he stay with us?"

Sylvie held her breath. *Ridge, please.*

"You're very good. Both of you." Ridge rose with obvious fatigue and lack of enthusiasm. "I just thought Ben needed a long-term solution. But I'll think over your offer and we'll talk tomorrow, okay? I'll be taking Ben home now."

A gloomy Ridge and a dejected Ben left almost immediately. Sylvie and her father stood, looking at the closed door for a long moment. Then Milo put his comforting arm around her shoulder. "Ridge is making a big mistake if he takes Ben away now."

*Another in a long line of mistakes,* Sylvie added silently. Was there any way to make Ridge see sense about Ben?

"Let's go to bed," her dad said. "I'm about to fall asleep on my feet. And we'll still be settling Rae-Jean and her baby in here tomorrow. It will be an adjustment for both of us having an infant in the house."

She nodded and he walked her to her bedroom door where he pecked her cheek good-night. *Lord, wake Ridge up and let him see Ben as a gift, not a burden.*

*March 8*

Late Tuesday afternoon, Sylvie paced the floor of the new clinic in Washburn. Her aunt Shirley was in the examination room with the nurse-practitioner who was examining Rae-Jean's baby girl, little Hope. What could go wrong next? Rae-Jean, looking exhausted and weak, had arrived home and Sylvie had put her to bed immediately.

And then she and Aunt Shirley had rushed the obviously very congested baby here. Just over five pounds in weight, tiny Hope had been born three weeks premature and was so fragile. And they still didn't know how the child would be affected from Rae-Jean's drug abuse the year before.

Then Aunt Shirley came out with the baby in her arms and smiled. "We just need to get a couple of prescriptions filled. And to pick up some camphorated oil."

Sylvie sighed with relief. Rae-Jean had a bad cold, too, and needed their attention.

A half hour later, Shirley parked in front of Milo's Bait and Tackle Shop. Two police cars were parked there. "Oh, no," Shirley moaned.

Sylvie knew just how her aunt felt. She was beginning to cringe at the sight of police vehicles. With a sinking feeling, she unhooked the baby from the car seat in the rear passenger compartment. And then both women hurried up the few steps to the shop. Milo, wearing a khaki quilted vest, met them at the shop's entrance.

"Dad, what's happened?" Sylvie asked, while Shirley cradled the blanket-shrouded baby close to protect her from the biting wind.

"I went to pick up a few groceries. While I was gone, someone got into our apartment and struck Rae-Jean from behind and knocked her out." Disbelief and anger colored each of his words. He took off his glasses to rub his eyes.

Sylvie shook her head as though trying to deny what had happened.

"Where is Rae-Jean, Milo?" Shirley asked, patting the fussing baby in her arms.

"That deputy, Trish, has driven her to the E.R. in

Ashford. I don't think she's hurt except for a lump and a bad headache."

The sound of footsteps sounded from above and then Ridge was there in front of them. "The sheriff would like you to come upstairs, please."

Ridge's unexpected presence jolted Sylvie's already jangled nerves. "You didn't get to take Ben to that school, did you?" His stark expression caused her to step back from him.

"I hadn't come to a decision yet," Ridge replied, shivering once from the cold. "Ben's in school today. Please, you need to come upstairs and look over your apartment." Without a further word, he turned and motioned them to precede him upstairs.

As she passed within inches of him, Sylvie could think of nothing either comforting or persuasive to say.

The sheriff was waiting for them in the kitchen. "Whoever broke in and struck Rae-Jean didn't have as much time to tear your place up as Ginger's apartment and your house." He nodded toward Shirley.

"You think there is just one person doing this?" Sylvie asked the sheriff. The unreality of someone breaking into their home and for an unknown reason was obviously shaking Sylvie's peace apart. "Is it just one person who is looking for something? But what?"

Keir shrugged, his features set in grim lines. Ridge stood at his side, reflecting the same mood in his expression and stance.

Sylvie wrapped her arms closer around the baby.

"Something will break," the sheriff said with what sounded like forced confidence. "This doesn't appear to be the work of a professional and he is bound to slip up, leave something behind. And we'll get him."

Shirley sank onto one of the kitchen chairs and unwrapped the thin blanket over the baby's head. She held the baby girl close and kissed her downy forehead. "What could they be looking for? And why? Oh, Lord, help us."

Sylvie's spirit echoed the despairing cry of Shirley's heart.

Keir asked Sylvie and Milo to make a cursory examination of places where they kept their extra cash and few valuables. Nothing was found missing and this didn't lighten the pervasive gloom. The sheriff asked them to wait downstairs in Milo's shop. But before she could comply, the kitchen phone rang. Sylvie picked it up and heard a voice over the line. "A lady is here who wants to dicker over the price of a book, one of the collectible editions of Georgette Heyer."

In her current mental fog, it took a few moments for Sylvie to understand who, where and what was happening. It was Shirley's neighbor Florence Levesque, who was watching Sylvie's shop for her today. "Florence, I'll come right over." She turned to Milo and Shirley and said, "I'll be right back."

When she walked outside, Ridge hailed her from the bottom of the steps, "Where are you going?"

"To my shop. Florence is there with a customer."

Ridge caught up with her. "I'll come with you." Without preamble, he continued as they walked side by side, "Do you have any idea at all of who might have done this?"

"None." Why was he coming with her? In spite of her limp, she found herself walking faster than usual in the brisk winter wind.

"Since I can't take Ben myself, I've decided I'm going to call a friend of mine in the Milwaukee Police Department and ask him to meet the bus from northern Wisconsin tomorrow. He can take Ben to the school. I don't know when I will be able to get away from this case. And I've got to get Ben to that school."

She cast him a scorching glance. "You're out of your mind," she declared, patience gone.

Ridge looked shocked. "What?"

"If you think that you can put Ben on a bus in Ashford tomorrow morning and that when it reaches Milwaukee that night, he will still be on it, you are out of your mind," she repeated.

Ridge made a sound of disgust. "You're right. I must be crazy to even think of doing that."

Most shops on the side street where they walked had been closed until spring. She had the haunting sensation that she was trudging through a ghost town with Ridge. The icy wind battered them, swirling particles of dry snow around their ankles.

Her hip ached from the cold and her indignation at his blind spot was fueling her weariness.

Suddenly she yearned for hot sun, green leaves, white sailboats on blue water and tourists shoulder to shoulder on this empty street, laughing and calling to each other. The fact that there was no escape, no way to leap ahead to the future where all the present problems and mysteries were solved sparked her temper.

She stopped and faced him. "You can't be any more frustrated than I am. I've lost Ginger. Some crazy person is going around tearing my family's houses apart searching for something. We don't know what that something is or how far they will go to get it. I mean, will they kill someone else?"

Before he could answer, she went on, feeling the tide of frustration roiling, frothing inside her. "And now Rae-Jean has been attacked. Just dealing with Rae-Jean coming home from prison with the baby would have been enough. You think you have problems? Both sides of my family are going through terrible times. You only have Ben to worry about and you seem totally unwilling to spend any time with the boy and be concerned about his problems."

"I have no experience with kids. But I'm trying to do the best I can. I wanted to get him settled so that he could have an easier time of it."

"Or maybe you could have an easier time of it? What is it about Ben that most makes you want to get rid of him? Is it because he's the same age as Dan was when he died?" she challenged him. Then that alarmed feeling shook her, warning her that she had gone too far.

Ridge made no reply. But he pulled away and began stalking the last few yards to the corner across from her bookshop.

She hurried after him; her hip faltered. She slipped on a patch of ice. And fell down hard.

Ridge turned back. "Are you all right?" He reached down to help her up from the icy pavement.

"I'm fine, but ashamed of myself." Her face blazed. She was usually so careful not to fall in order not to aggravate her damaged hip further. And usually so careful of others' feelings. "Ridge, I'm ashamed of myself for my anger at you. But I'm so concerned about Ben and his needs." She couldn't look him in the eye. "He's so fragile at this time."

Ridge drew her to her feet. One of his hands cupped her neck under her collar. The satiny fabric sensitized her neck or was it that his hand was only a millimeter from her skin?

"Don't give it a thought." His voice was still rough, but diffident. "After the past five days, neither of us has any patience or nerves left. And I don't seem to be making a lot of good decisions about Ben." His other hand pressed against the small of her back, drawing her closer to him, evidently keeping her steady. "With all that's happened over the past few days, it's a wonder we're still in our right minds."

"Maybe I'm not," she teased a bit, trying to make up for goading him, striking him when he was already down. "I'm so sorry, Ridge," she whispered.

Regret again triggered the tears that had hovered just a breath away from the moment she'd found Ginger dead. "I'm so sorry—" she blinked away the tears "—I just wish I could help you. Help Ben… Help you see that he has needs and feelings and…" All the emotions of the day, of the week overcame her. And then her head was resting against his chest again. The wool of his coat rasped her cheek.

He didn't speak. He didn't move. But he held her close. And that was what she needed now. No one had held her like this for a very long time. As winter dusk turned the sky to pewter, the last of the day's wind continued to flog them. His nearness began to settle deep into her, soothing all of the ruffled edges that the last few days had caused.

Finally his voice came soft and low. "Sylvie, there is a reason that all this happened. Something that Ginger said or did or saw made her a target. Someone knows that Tom and Shirley were her parents and that you were her cousin and close friend. So both your houses were places that she might have visited the night she came home."

"Or that she might have stayed last fall when she

finished her summer here and left for Alaska again?" She looked up.

"That's right. These three places—her apartment, her parents' home and your apartment—all were places she would have been last summer." His voice gained momentum. "What happened to Ginger last summer that would have carried over until now?" He stepped away from her.

She sensed him reestablishing his distance from her. Their moment of closeness was over. "But why would someone wait until now? Wouldn't it have been easier to investigate, search these places, especially Ginger's apartment, after she left for Alaska and before she came home?"

"Good point. But it leads nowhere." He dropped his hands from her.

Bereft of his touch, she said, "I still think we need to find out what her surprise was. Maybe she told someone else around here. Maybe someone she knew met her when she came to town and told her something."

"A better point." His businesslike manner had returned, searing their connection. "We've asked that anyone who has information about Ginger's movements the night she came home to come forward. No one has but you."

"But if they have a guilty secret, they wouldn't come forward," she said, reestablishing her independence, too. She couldn't let herself depend on

Ridge. His stay here would be fleeting. "Because they would still be looking for whatever she had that they want…"

"Yes, and we don't know what that is. But can you think of anyplace in Winfield or nearby that she frequented last summer that might be a hiding place for something important?" He studied her as though he could summon the answer from her with a word.

Blocking Ridge out so she could concentrate, Sylvie closed her eyes and tried to think. Ginger had worked the excursion boats that toured the Apostle Islands. That led nowhere. She shook her head.

"Can you think of anywhere that she stopped before she came to you that first night?"

Sylvie replayed in her mind the evening with Ginger and then the night she and her father had found Ben in Ginger's attic. The peanut butter that Ben had eaten—yes. "Groceries. She had bought groceries."

"Groceries? You mean the ones in Ginger's fridge?"

"Yes."

"I thought one of the deputies, that young one, Josh, told me you'd put those groceries in the fridge."

"No, Ginger bought them."

"Bought them here—locally?" His voice lifted with increasing interest. "Or on her way home?"

Sylvie shook her head. "I don't know."

"We'll have to find out."

Sylvie looked up into his face. They were still so close together. The chill temperature had worked its way over her face, down her neck, and was trying to snake its way deeper inside her. But she had no desire to go in out of the cold. She was content to stand here quietly, looking at Ridge. For once, he didn't look stressed. Just in the midst of intense concentration.

"Hey! Sylvie!" Florence called from across the street. "Aren't you going to come and sell this lady a book?"

Sylvie hurried across the street.

Ridge hung back, watching her go. No matter this lead about the groceries, he had rarely felt so incompetent. Since he'd come to town, three houses had been broken into and ransacked, one woman had been killed and now one had been assaulted. When would they solve this puzzle?

Ridge had appreciated the sheriff's show of confidence earlier but how many more times would it take before this case was solved? And he understood Sylvie's concern that before they did, someone else might get killed.

# FOUR

*March 11*

On Friday afternoon, Ridge sat adjacent to Keir in the bare interrogation room. He had a prickly feeling up his spine. He didn't know if it was from all the tension over the past few days or if it was because he wanted to shake the young woman across the table from him.

At the small scarred wooden table, Tanya Hendricks sat in an odd posture. Her chair sat back a foot or so from the table. She'd slid her bottom very far forward on the seat; her head was bent forward and her arms were folded over her very thin chest. One long leg crossed the other. The leg on top jittered, broadcasting her nervous strain.

On two previous occasions, Keir and Ridge had stopped to interview her at her grandfather's home where she was staying. But she seemed to elude them. So they had at last formally called her in to answer questions about Ginger's stop at Ollie's convenience store on the way into Winfield on the night Ginger died.

Tanya was tall, painfully thin, with long, dirty-brown hair. She wore what appeared to be designer clothes that she didn't take care of very well and probably couldn't afford to replace. Her wrinkled white blouse looked as if it had shrunk. Her Armani denim jeans were stained and threadbare.

And she had an attitude. A bad one.

As the sheriff questioned her, Ridge paid little attention to the lies and evasions she was giving him. She had a habit of letting her voice drop until her words could hardly be discerned. She rarely raised her eyes above the tabletop. He wished they were videotaping her. She would have made a good case study for police trainees in spotting an untrustworthy witness. And a suspected drug user.

"Miss Hendricks," the sheriff said, sounding as if his patience was about to give way, "we watched the surveillance videotape from the night in question. And Ginger Johnson was definitely in the store buying groceries from you that night. Now what did she say to you?"

"You know, the usual…" Tanya shrugged, still not meeting the sheriff's eyes.

"The usual what?"

Ridge didn't hear her reply. He tried to temper

his irritation with this difficult witness. "Did she say anything about just getting back to town?" he asked, finally entering into the interrogation.

Tanya gave her customary insolent shrug once more. "It was nothing special, you know. Just the usual garb…"

"Garbage?" he finished for her. "Ginger looked quite animated on the video." Ridge wondered why Tanya was being evasive. Perhaps it was just her personality; maybe she acted this way with every adult in every situation. Or maybe it was that they were law enforcement or "pigs." He didn't know much about this girl. He vaguely remembered Ollie's very pretty daughter, this girl's mother, who had been a few years ahead of him in school. But that was all.

"I don't know what that means. What's animated? It sounds like a cartoon," the girl complained, rolling her eyes.

"She looked happy." Keir's voice remained even. "She looked like she was saying a lot to you."

Not for the first time, Ridge wished that surveillance videos also had an audio band. Then they wouldn't have to interview this surly teenager.

"I don't listen to people anymore." The girl began to nibble a hangnail. "I just ring…their purchases and take their money, give them change. That's all I do. No matter what my granddad says. I'm not responsible—" The girl again muttered so low Ridge had a hard time hearing her. "—buying…not pick-ing…lottery tickets."

"Please speak up. Was anyone with Ginger?" Ridge asked, just fishing for anything, nothing in particular. "Maybe somebody who didn't come in with her, but who was waiting outside for her?"

"I didn't see anybody. But I…looking, you know what I mean? Work is so…so lame. I just try to get through it. I don't pay much attention."

If she'd been his daughter, Ridge would have grounded her until she could learn to speak up and speak respectfully to police officers. However, he clamped his mouth shut.

Keir gave him a glance that said he didn't have anything more to ask her. Did Ridge?

Ridge shook his head. He rose, as did the sheriff. Keir said, "You may leave, then, Miss Hendricks. Thank you for your help." Still slouching, she slunk toward the door.

Just as she was going through, Ridge called to her, "You let us know if anything occurs to you, won't you?"

She glanced over her shoulder and gave him a dirty look that said clearly, *In your dreams.* Then she was gone with a slam of the outer door.

Ridge's cell phone rang. He answered it. And a deep frown creased his forehead as he listened to his last hope vanishing. He kept his conversation polite, then snapped the phone shut.

"Miss Hendricks was not a very good witness," Keir said wryly, stating the obvious and bringing Ridge back to the just-completed interrogation.

"She's probably too high most of the time to catch what's going on around her," Ridge said with a frown. "What was that last part about lottery tickets? I thought you had to be eighteen in order to sell them."

"She just turned eighteen, I think. And Ollie, her grandfather, often has tourists who buy a winning lottery ticket, but don't turn it in to get their prize. If the winner doesn't turn in the ticket, the vendor doesn't get his percentage of the prize. A big one worth several million was bought at his store last fall and no one picked it up."

"A winning lottery ticket," Ridge said, suddenly alert. "Is there any chance that Ginger might have bought a winning ticket?"

"I don't see Shirley Johnson's daughter buying lottery tickets, do you?" Keir shook his head. "Besides, Ginger was gone and in Alaska before this particular ticket was sold. I think it may have already expired. Or is just about to."

Everything Keir said hit the mark. No, Ridge didn't see Shirley Johnson's daughter buying a lottery ticket. The Patterson family didn't hold with gambling, not even buying lottery tickets. Shirley and Milo's father had gambled away acres of choice property around Winfield, a cautionary lesson for succeeding generations like Ginger. *I must be desperate. I'm really grabbing at straws.* Why couldn't they get a break in this case?

"Anyway," Keir promised, "I'm going to keep an eye on Tanya Hendricks. If nothing else, maybe I can pick up a new supplier in the area. I wonder if Ollie knows his granddaughter is likely using drugs."

Then Keir's cell phone rang, interrupting them. He opened it and began speaking to his wife. He said goodbye to her and then he looked at Ridge. "I'm done here. I'm going with Audra for an ultrasound. The doctor thinks she might be expecting twins."

Ridge nodded. "Fine. I've got to go now. I'm moving Ben to Milo's apartment today after school."

"The military school fell through?"

"Yes, that was them on the phone. They've given the vacancy to the next boy on the waiting list. They've put Ben on the list for next fall." But Ridge wondered if that would ever happen. Maybe Ben needed someone like Milo. Still, he couldn't shift the responsibility of Ben to Milo.

"I'm sorry that this case has interfered with your private plans for your ward," Keir apologized.

The words didn't change things, but they made Ridge feel somewhat better. "It's not your fault. It's the fault of the person who—by accident or design—pushed Ginger to her death."

The sheriff nodded gravely. "We're going to nail him or her. No matter what it takes."

Ben was waiting for Ridge in the doorway of his parents' house. "I'm all packed up and ready to go." The kid was actually dancing from foot to foot with his eagerness to leave.

Ridge identified with Ben; he shared the same reaction to this cold, empty house. If only he could move into Milo's, too. "Let's go check your room just to be sure that you haven't forgotten anything."

With dragging feet, Ben followed him through the kitchen to the hallway that led to the bedrooms. Ben waited impatiently in the doorway as Ridge looked through the vacant closet, through the empty drawers of the dresser. "Did you get down and look under the bed?"

With a hiss of impatience, Ben threw himself onto his stomach beside the bed and looked underneath. "Nothing. Can we go now?"

Ridge nodded. Ben raced up the hall ahead of him and stopped at the back door just to pull on his winter jacket and hat. The kid swung his school duffel bag over one shoulder and then picked up the smaller suitcase. He waited for Ridge.

For just a moment, Ridge considered taking Ben to his mom in front of the TV set, and having the kid thank her for her hospitality. Then the reality of the situation poked him hard. All his mom and dad wanted was Ben out of their house. So why put on an act? The kid hadn't been fooled. He'd clearly read the situation as it was.

Feeling that he should apologize to Ben for making him spend months here, Ridge shouldered a box of Ben's possessions and picked up the larger suitcase. Once they were in Ridge's SUV, he drove the few blocks to Milo's Bait and Tackle Shop.

He'd barely turned off the engine and Ben was already charging up the steps to the apartment above the store. When Ridge reached the top step, Ben was there in the doorway, waiting for him. "The note on my bed says that after I put my stuff in my room, I'm to come downstairs. Milo wants me to learn where everything is so I can help customers this spring and summer."

"I'm sure," Ridge said, leading Ben through the kitchen and living room to one of the bedrooms at the rear, "that Milo wants you to do more than just throw everything in a heap in the middle of the room."

Ben groaned with frustration. But with Ridge giving him directions, he put away the underwear and socks into the new set of dresser drawers. Ridge's mom had washed, carefully folded and packed them. Ridge was glad for this show of concern for Ben. Ben placed his school duffel bag on his desk by the window. "Can I go now? Milo needs me."

Ridge relented. "You go on. You can finish up later."

Ben was gone in a nanosecond.

Ridge stood in the bedroom for a few moments, thinking about his plans for Ben and how they had gone awry. He pushed these thoughts aside and walked toward the kitchen door to leave.

The door opened and Sylvie walked in. "Oh!"

She looked like a snow princess. Her white-blond bangs peeked out from under an angora knit tam. The eye-catching tam matched the plum coat and leather gloves. In an area where most everyone wore flannel and denim, Sylvie always dressed with style.

"Hi," was all he could manage to say. His mouth had gone a little dry.

She swept off her knit tam and then ruffled her close-cropped hair.

He stepped forward and helped her out of her long coat and hung it up on one of the pegs by the door. She slipped her gloves into its pocket and then rubbed her hands together. "Please tell me spring is coming. Someday. Soon."

He tried to smile. But she was so lovely standing there in the low light with her silvery-blond hair gleaming and her cheeks rosy pink from the cold. She was wearing one of her colorful, intricate hand-knit Fair Isle sweaters and light blue corduroy slacks. He couldn't find a word to say to her.

She glanced downward.

Did she think he was perturbed with her because he'd been unable to take Ben to the military school?

"I take it that Ben has brought his stuff over?" Her voice was subdued.

"Yes." What was wrong with him? Why couldn't he say more than one-syllable words to her today? He'd never had trouble speaking with Sylvie in the past.

She looked up, her expression and violet eyes grave. "I'm glad you've come. I wanted to talk over all that has happened about Ginger's death, the investigation, and find out if any progress has been made."

"I'll tell you what I'm at liberty to reveal."

She nodded solemnly. "Have you decided yet whether Rae-Jean was attacked just because she was in the wrong place at the wrong time or whether someone wanted to hurt or kill her?"

"The sheriff and I agree that she was in the wrong place at the wrong time. Unless something develops later on that supposition which may cause of us to change our opinion."

She motioned him toward the table and chair. "I got an interesting and troubling phone call today."

"From whom?" He remained standing, unwilling to stay here alone with her. Why was it different between them this time? Why did she draw his attention in this way? She'd always been pretty. He'd always been fond of her but what was different now?

"Please sit down," she said. "I'll make us some hot cocoa." She turned toward the stove and soon had milk warming in a saucepan. "It was from the assistant professor that Ginger was dating."

Ridge sat down reluctantly and now his gaze followed her movements. He couldn't stop himself from asking, "What did he call about?"

"He said that he had been thinking about Ginger." She stirred generous spoonfuls of chocolate Ovaltine into the warm milk. "Hearing that her death had been deemed suspicious caused him to think over some events he felt were disturbing. Things that had happened in the past year."

"What did happen over the past year?" Ridge felt his interest quicken in spite of his skepticism.

Sylvie set a mug of fragrant hot cocoa in front of him and sat down across from him with another cup for herself. She folded her hands around the mug, very tense. "He said that there had been an ugly incident in Alaska late last fall."

"Ugly—how?"

"I don't know if you realize it but there is an extreme strain of environmentalists—people like the Unabomber."

He lifted his mug and took a sip—sweet and hot. "That insane guy that blew up things in the eighties?"

"Yes, there are environmentalists who are rabidly against testing anything on animals, no matter what kind of makeup or medicine it is and no matter how carefully protected the animals are. And these activists are vehemently against the eating of meat or the processing of hides." She looked at him over the rim of her mug. "They're called ELF."

"Elf?" Was she putting him on? No, of course not. Not about Ginger.

"Yes, the Earth Liberation Front. They're also called ecoterrorists."

He again resisted saying that she must be making the name ELF up. But if Sylvie said there was an ELF organization, there was. "I've heard of ecoterrorists," he admitted.

"Well, these militant activists can get violent. They have attacked people who raise cattle for food or minks for fur."

"I remember hearing about a mink farm in Iowa," Ridge said, pulling this up from memory. "Some environmentalist nutcase came and released all the mink from their cages and the poor little creatures got smashed on the highway. Pointless and cruel."

"That's the kind of thing that they do." Sylvie put her mug down and traced the rim with one finger. "They aren't rational people like normal environmentalists. And in this case, evidently this particular fanatic had confused Ginger with another G. Johnson who is doing research on new uses for fish by-products."

He followed the movement of her slender index finger as it circled the lip of the mug. Completely captivated. "Are you making this up?"

"I wish I were." She lowered her hand and

sighed. "This animal-rights terrorist spray-painted her name and threats in neon orange on the outside of the research building where she was doing some work for another professor. The FBI interviewed her about it because this extremist had previously tried to kill two technicians at a California lab where pharmaceuticals were being tested on animals."

"The FBI?" This must be for real. He leaned forward. "Did this assistant professor recall the name of this particular crazy?"

Sylvie reached in her sweater pocket and pulled out a slip of paper. "I wrote it down for you. I thought you could get more information through official channels." She handed it to him.

His fingers brushed hers. Had he done that on purpose? Or had she? He read the paper, but the name meant nothing to him. Still, he would definitely investigate it. "Exactly what research was Ginger doing in Alaska?"

"I don't understand all of it. But she was investigating transient killer whales in the waters around Alaska." She leaned back and folded her arms as if preparing to defend herself. "The most famous of these are six that are called the Kodiak Killers."

Again, if anyone other than Sylvie had been telling him this, he would have doubted her veracity. He couldn't keep doubt from entering his voice. "The Kodiak Killers?"

"Yes, there is a band of six killer whales that

spend part of their winters around the city of Kodiak." She took up her mug for another sip. "They're unusual because they seem to specialize in hunting a certain type of sea lion, Stellar sea lions, and eating them. Very successfully, I hear."

"The Kodiak Killers?" Ridge repeated, watching her sip the hot cocoa. Her every move was elegant and graceful, even this everyday act.

"Yes. Ginger, along with other scientists, was studying why they pick on Stellar sea lions and if the depredations of these particular sea lions will seriously endanger the sea lions' numbers."

Ridge suddenly felt his respect for Ginger Johnson increasing. And also regret that her work had been cut short. "So Ginger's boyfriend thinks this fanatic might have followed her here?"

"He says it might be him or someone else like him." She glanced into Ridge's eyes. "The ELF group is disorganized but is active on the Internet. So some deranged environmentalist here might have picked up the same incorrect information and targeted Ginger."

"But," Ridge asked, "what would he be ransacking her apartment and other homes for?"

"Perhaps he wanted to destroy her research on her computer. And also computer CDs that might contain her records and her research?" Sylvie offered. "When I asked her assistant professor what someone would be looking for among Ginger's possessions, that's the only thing he could think of. He was surprised by all the break-ins. He said it really didn't make any sense. But I suppose if we are dealing with irrational people that we could expect them to do irrational acts."

"Even irrational people make sense on some level." Still he shook his head. He was baffled and he might as well admit it. "I don't know where this will all end up."

The wall phone near her head rang. Sylvie reached out and lifted the receiver to her ear. Shock and dismay flashed over her features. She stood up. "I'll be right over. And I'll bring Ridge with me."

"What is it?" he demanded, standing.

"Doyle Keski, Chad's dad, has burst into Shirley's house uninvited. Chad, Shirley and Rae-Jean are there alone." She was already pulling on her long coat and opening the door.

"I'll call the police," Ridge said, following her and reaching for his cell phone.

"No," Sylvie said, running down the steps. "Shirley called here for Milo. Tom's out gathering food for the local food pantry. She wanted Milo to come and run Keski off. She doesn't want to call the police unless absolutely necessary. She doesn't want Chad embarrassed by having his father's name in the paper under Local Arrests. Again."

# FIVE

Instead of running the few blocks, Ridge insisted that he drive Sylvie in his vehicle. If Doyle Keski had assaulted someone at Shirley and Tom's house and needed to be arrested, it would make it so much easier just to drag him out and drive him to the sheriff's office. When he pulled to a halt in front of Shirley's Victorian, Sylvie leaped out ahead of him and ran awkwardly, painfully, toward the house. Ridge charged after her, gaining on her, pushing in front of her at the door to protect her. Didn't she have enough sense to stay out of a violent confrontation? "Stay back," he ordered.

The front door flew open and there stood Shirley, a sweater around her shoulders. Up the front staircase, Rae-Jean, with the baby in her arms, waited, huddled against the foyer wall. "Thank heavens, you've come!" Shirley exclaimed. "Chad's father just barged in and he won't leave. He's cornered Chad in the kitchen."

Ridge shouldered past the women. Following the sound of an agitated male voice, he found his way to the kitchen toward the rear. In spite of all his years away from Winfield, he recognized Doyle Keski immediately. The short, wiry troublemaker was wearing a dirty flannel shirt, an ancient CPO jacket and ragged jeans. He reeked of liquor. He was shouting at a teenager whom he'd backed against the wall. Ridge recognized the kid as Shirley's foster son, Chad Keski.

"You're still my kid!" Doyle yelled.

How like this bully to attack a house of women and children. Ridge clamped his hand on Keski's shoulder. "You were not invited to enter this private home—" Ridge began.

Keski turned, his fist drawn back.

Ridge expected this. He was ready. He grabbed Keski's wrist and twisted it hard, halting the punch. He increased pressure around the shorter man's wrist, forcing a gasp from Keski. Ridge then grasped Keski's shoulder, pinching the man's trapezius muscle, exerting painful pressure there. This made it impossible for Keski to raise his other fist. And gave Ridge a great deal of satisfaction.

Keski bent forward with the pain; his face twisted into an agonized grimace. "Let…go…of me."

Instead, Ridge increased his pressure on Keski's wrist and trapezius. "As soon as you join me outside in the backyard, I'll release you."

Keski struggled to end Ridge's hold on him. He grunted with exertion. But he couldn't break free.

Inexorably Ridge began to propel the resisting, cursing man toward the back door out of Shirley's kitchen.

The back door burst open in front of them and Chaney Franklin, Rae-Jean's estranged husband, filled the doorway. He was a mountain of a man— literally. "What's the trouble here?"

Ridge did not get a chance to answer. Neither did Keski.

"You!" Chaney boomed. He grabbed Keski from Ridge's grasp by the scruff of the neck. Yanked him like a whimpering puppy out onto the back porch.

Not to be left behind, Ridge clung to Keski's wrist and hurried forward, staying on his feet. Outside, the three of them reached the bottom of the back steps onto the narrow shoveled walk. There, Ridge asserted his authority. "I'm a law officer, Chaney. I'll handle this."

Chaney looked disgruntled. But he released Keski, who staggered with his sudden release. Chaney took a step back.

"Keski, I don't know why you are here bothering these people," Ridge growled. "But you're guilty of trespassing and disturbing the peace. Leave now and don't return without an invitation." Then with a shove, he released Keski from his grasp.

Stumbling, Doyle cursed him and then shoulder-bumped Chaney on his way to the back alley.

Ridge and Chaney stood, watching as the man climbed into his old rust bucket truck and roared away down the alley. Ridge found himself breathing hard. He looked up at the tall man opposite him. "Where did you come from?"

"On my way to work. Just stopped to say hi to my kid. He stays with Florence after school." Chaney nodded toward Florence Lévesque's house next door. "Heard the commotion. Glad I did, although I guess you had everything under control."

Ridge shook off his leftover antagonism and offered his hand. "Thanks for your help."

"No problem." Chaney shook his hand.

"Are you two all right?" Sylvie called from the back door. She'd followed Ridge but had kept her distance. Not wanting to get in his way. She'd been so afraid that there would be violence. And was so grateful Ridge had handled it.

"Is that you, Chaney?" Her cousin Rae-Jean stood right behind Sylvie with little Hope in her arms.

"You get back inside, Rae-Jean," Chaney instructed her. "You two have been sick." The large man with reddish hair hurried up the steps.

Sylvie stepped out of the way to let him go in. The protective tone in Chaney Franklin's voice warmed her heart.

Ridge followed Chaney up the steps. She didn't move out of his way. There was so much she wanted to say. Couldn't say.

He paused abreast of her, his gaze linked to hers. She understood the question in his eyes without his asking it. Everyone in town knew that Rae-Jean's baby had been conceived during a troubled time in her marriage to Chaney and that, though separated, they were legally still married. Everyone also knew that Rae-Jean didn't know whether Hope's father was Chaney or not. "We need to let the sheriff know that Doyle Keski is back in town," she said as Ridge escorted her through the enclosed back porch.

And suddenly she wondered how long Doyle Keski had been back in town. Could it possibly be Doyle who was responsible for the break-ins? Now, however, was not the time to bring this up to Ridge in front of everyone.

She shivered from being out in the cold. Or perhaps it was residual reaction to violence. The narrow, brightly lit kitchen was crowded with family and friends. So Sylvie stood in the background next to Ridge.

"I still think someone should have called the sheriff," Ridge muttered from his place by her side.

Shirley was standing near Chad, who had slumped onto a chair at the narrow kitchen table. As if she'd heard him, Shirley looked to Ridge and then to Chad and then back to Ridge.

Sylvie touched Ridge's sleeve and whispered, "I don't think Shirley wants to cause a complete breach between Doyle and Chad. Doyle *is* Chad's father."

Frowning, Ridge shook his head at her and took a step forward. "Chad—" Ridge's expression became austere and his tone gritty "—your father should not be allowed to just barge in here whenever he feels like it and threaten people."

Chad looked at Ridge. The room got very quiet. "We should call the sheriff," Chad said. "Tom told me not to fight with my dad. But I don't want him coming around here and upsetting everybody. And he just does it to be mean. He doesn't care about me."

Sylvie looked to her aunt Shirley and saw that Chad's words were a huge relief to her in one way. And heartbreaking in another.

"I'll call the sheriff, then," Ridge offered. "I think you should get a restraining order, too, Shirley. That should keep Keski away."

"And maybe with everything that's been going on around Winfield," Chaney added darkly, "I think we should discuss getting a security system installed here. After all, Rae-Jean and the baby are staying here and sometimes our boy. I'd be happy to chip in."

"I think Tom would agree," Shirley said.

Rae-Jean gave a weak smile and then sat down at the table with the baby in her arms. "It's all so scary." Her faint voice shook.

Over the phone, Ridge explained to the sheriff's

dispatch about Doyle Keski's trespass and the dispatcher said someone would be coming soon to take down their information about the incident. The woman also suggested that Shirley and Tom take out a restraining order against Doyle Keski.

From Rae-Jean's arms, Chaney had lifted the baby girl, maybe his baby girl, and was talking to her in a gentle voice. Seeing such a large man holding such a tiny child with such care brought a wave of tenderness, which threatened to overwhelm Sylvie. And Chaney didn't even know for sure this was his child. Would she ever have a baby who was loved by the father like this?

"I think that both a restraining order and security system," Ridge commented, "might be very good ideas."

Sylvie felt him rest his hand on her shoulder. His wordless comfort caught her around the heart. She glanced at her aunt Shirley's face and caught from her a look of caution.

Moving from Ridge's touch, Sylvie drifted to the stove and began making a fresh pot of coffee. Her aunt was right. She couldn't get comfortable having Ridge protecting her. Safeguarding others was just his nature. And she shouldn't read anything more into it.

*March 13*

Two days later in the gloomy late-winter afternoon, Ridge sat beside the sheriff in his Jeep. They were on their way to Jim Leahy's summer house, east of town along the shore of Superior. They were going to either find Leahy in residence or if not, execute a search warrant to see what was going on in the house, the house that should have been quiet and empty at this time of the year.

"Tom came in and applied for a restraining order against Doyle Keski yesterday," Keir said.

"Glad to hear it." Ridge's mind returned to the memory of Sylvie gracefully and quietly moving around Shirley's kitchen, serving coffee and tea. And it prompted another line of inquiry he'd planned to discuss today. "Did Sylvie call you about speaking to the assistant professor who was dating Ginger?"

"No, I haven't heard from her. What's this about?" Keir glanced sideways.

"Maybe she felt funny about telling you since her information was pretty ambiguous. But I contacted the FBI and talked to one of their Midwest experts on ecoterrorism."

"Ecoterrorism?" Keir's tone was incredulous. "In Winfield?"

"Yes, to cut to the chase, some fringe extremist-environmentalist harassed and threatened Ginger at a research lab in the Northwest. Seems he confused her with another G. Johnson who was testing animals or something."

"And you think this fanatic may have followed her here?" Keir's skeptical tone hadn't changed.

Ridge tried not to get defensive. "Either that or maybe some other unbalanced activist got the same misinformation and maybe went a little too far."

"And killed Ginger by accident?" The sheriff shrugged. "I suppose it's possible," he finished, still sounding unconvinced.

"The FBI ecoterrorism expert seemed to think it could explain what happened to Ginger, especially since her computer was taken," Ridge continued, presenting what he and the FBI had put together. "When the fanatic didn't find the evidence of Ginger's suspect research in the laptop files, he might still be looking for CDs with her research on them."

"But why?" Keir lifted a palm.

"So no one else can use her research. To hurt innocent animals." Keir's continued skepticism was getting on Ridge's nerves. He loosened his neck muscles by stretching forward and to each side.

"So killing a research scientist is okay if it's to protect animals. It is a strange world we live in today," Keir observed drily.

"I won't disagree with you. I can't." Ridge kept his eyes looking ahead. He was glad to drop Ginger's complicated case for a simpler one. "We're just about there, aren't we?"

"Yes, I wanted to come myself and bring you along because it's very touchy entering the house of a summer resident—even with a search warrant. Having a state detective with me puts me in a stronger position legally. Plus two deputies will meet us before we go onto the property. We don't know exactly what we will find. We could find nothing. Or we could stumble onto a meth lab." The sheriff's tone was ominous.

"From what you told me," Ridge said as they drove between mounds of brown-tinged snow, piled up on both sides of the highway, "it sounds as if something has changed at this place. You said Leahy rarely comes to his seasonal house except for four months in the summer."

"Yes, a neighbor who lives here year-round called in that he kept seeing car lights, driving onto and off the property at all times of the day and night. That sounds suspicious. We couldn't just call Leahy to check on him because his phone's disconnected for the winter. I've sent deputies out here twice to knock on the door. But no one has answered them. So I had no choice. I have to look into it."

"Or you'd be culpable for not checking out something suspicious," Ridge agreed.

Keir inhaled deeply. "Yes, especially with all these home break-ins and Ginger's death. I just can't take anything lightly."

The sheriff slowed on the two-lane highway, approaching the house in question. "Well, someone has plowed his drive recently. But many homeowners pay to have this done throughout the winter just in case they come up." The sheriff turned and drove up the narrow lane, carved through the deep, pristine white snow.

Behind them, another sheriff's Jeep turned off the highway and followed them in to the cleared turnaround near the garage of an impressive two-story log home.

Keir, Ridge, Trish and another younger deputy, Josh, got out with their sidearms ready. Keir nodded to Trish and Josh, who circled through the deep snow around to the front of the house, which faced Lake Superior. Ridge followed Keir to the back door, which opened toward the highway they'd just traveled. Keir knocked on the door with his search warrant in one hand.

No one answered. Keir knocked louder. And then louder. And then he shouted, "Mr. Leahy! Jim Leahy, this is the sheriff! Please open up! I have a search warrant!"

The sound of a dog barking inside was disconcerting. Someone must be staying in the house. But convinced no one was going to answer, Ridge was sizing up the knob and dead bolt locks, so they would know what to tell the locksmith.

Then the door opened. "What do you want?" a disheveled man shouted at them. A small white dog frisking around the man's ankles continued yapping at them.

Instinctively Ridge tensed and gripped the Glock in his hand.

The sheriff replied calmly, "I am Keir Harding, Winfield County Sheriff, and I have a search warrant to inspect your house."

"Search warrant?" the man snarled. And then he looked down. "Shut up!" he shouted at the dog. The dog looked insulted and then flopped down.

"This is the Leahy home, isn't it?" Keir asked. "Are you Jim Leahy, the owner?"

"Yeah," the man replied belligerently. "So what?"

"Do you have a government-issued picture ID that can prove that?" Keir asked.

"I'm Jim Leahy. This is my home. Get off my property."

"I can insist on seeing identification, sir. I need to know if you have the right to be on these premises. If you are Jim Leahy, why would you object to showing me your driver's license? I am here to protect your property."

The man swore at them with a long line of vulgar insults. He slammed the door. Within moments, he was back with his wallet open. He shoved it in the sheriff's face. "Here. Are you happy?"

The sheriff took hold of the wallet, which was opened to reveal a driver's license under clear plastic. The man did not release it. The sheriff took his time examining the ID. "Thank you, Mr. Leahy."

"Get off my land," Leahy said.

"Mr. Leahy, one of your neighbors noticed unusual activity around your home and reported it. It is my job to protect the property of all of our residents both year-round and seasonal."

Leahy slammed the door in their faces.

The sheriff radioed the two officers on the other side of the house to return to their vehicle and leave the area. It was a false alarm. The owner was at the house.

Back in the Jeep, Ridge looked over at the sheriff and voiced the question on both their minds, "What's his problem?"

"Something fishy is going on," the sheriff replied. "Seasonal residents are usually happy to see that we're keeping a close watch on their property while they're gone. Something here isn't right. Something is suspicious. And I'm going to keep an eye on Mr. Leahy."

That evening, Ridge felt distinctly out of his element. It was Parents' Night at Ben's middle school. Alongside Sylvie and Milo, Ridge was following Ben as he diffidently showed them his homeroom, his desk, and led them to his work on the bulletin boards all around the room where exemplary papers from students were displayed. Ridge didn't know exactly how to act. A few of the A+ papers belonged to Ben. Should he speak encouragingly or would Ben prefer him to remain silent?

Then he realized that he didn't really need to say anything because Milo was doing a very good job with Ben. This did not reassure Ridge. *He is my ward. I should be learning how to speak to him.* He shoved his frustration aside. And it was so easy to step back and let Milo, who obviously knew how to handle kids, take over. This was not the time or place to decide what to do with Ben or himself for that matter. Besides, it was so pleasant to stand near Sylvie and let Milo and Sylvie ask the right questions.

Sylvie kept track of Ridge's taciturn expression. He walked beside her through the narrow aisles around desks in Ben's classroom. She'd tried to mind her own business in regard to Ridge and Ben. But maybe she was wrong. Maybe God had brought Ridge back to make him face the past once and for all.

Other parents and family members already clogged the aisles, causing her to walk single file and very close to Ridge. A few times when she had been bumped, she had been forced to grip his shoulder to keep her balance. She was very aware of him tonight in this unusual setting. And she was very aware of several in the room who appeared to take an interest in noticing Ridge was with her. Didn't her father's presence tell them that this was a "family" outing?

Finally, the crowd swelled and she and Ridge found themselves pushed out into the hallway. "Why don't we get a jump on the crowd and get a cup of coffee and a cookie in the cafeteria now?" he suggested, obviously ready to leave the gathering behind.

"Let me ask my dad if he and Ben are ready, too."

But Milo and Ben had begun talking to Ben's wood shop teacher and told them to go on ahead. So they walked the polished linoleum floor of the old school where they both had attended. Most of the parents were still in the classrooms and they could hear the rumble of voices as they passed each opened classroom door. Finally she couldn't stop herself. "What's wrong?" she asked him.

"Thinking about the case I'm working on and also about going with Keir with the warrant the other day."

"Do you mean when the two of you went out to Leahy's place?"

"Winfield's communication grapevine is still in good working order, isn't it?" His tone was dry.

She ignored his comment. "There is something else you might want to know about Jim Leahy."

"What?"

"You remember questioning that girl who worked at Ollie's convenience store? Tanya Hendricks? Jim Leahy's her stepfather. Or was. Her mother divorced Leahy last year and married someone else, someone more well-heeled than Leahy is. That's why Tanya is here with Ollie." The two of them turned a corner, leaving the noise behind them.

"The new stepfather didn't want a package deal, so Tanya was sent back here to Ollie, her grandfather."

"Why do you mention this sad story to me?"

"Because I know you had questioned Tanya in connection with Ginger buying groceries at Ollie's the night she arrived in Winfield." Their footsteps fell quietly in the empty hallway.

"Is everyone keeping as close a track on this investigation as you are or is it just because this is about your cousin?" he asked, sounding peeved.

His tone prodded her like a pointed stick. "I don't know. But I do know it is painfully important to me to find out who killed my cousin and why. And more to the point, if it was planned or just an accident." She pulled a little way from him.

"I'm sorry. I wasn't being very sensitive." He touched her arm and then let go.

"That's okay." She realized that, as a law officer, he saw things differently than she did. "Nothing has been going right for anyone this year." She shrugged. "Or sometimes that's how it feels."

"You're right, nothing has been going well. I don't mean to take it out on you. But being here, back in that house…" He turned half away from her.

She took courage from his mentioning his father and mother. Maybe this was the opening to speak of the past. "They've never gotten over losing Dan. Do you know why? I've always wondered."

Evidently seeking privacy, he pulled her just

inside an empty classroom. "If we're asking questions," he said, "why haven't you ever had your hip operated on, corrected?"

She sighed over his maneuvering her away from his parents' dilemma. She settled onto the nearby teacher's wooden desktop. "When I was younger, they wanted to fuse my hip but I didn't want that. And when hip replacements became a possibility, the doctors told me I must wait until I couldn't walk at all."

"Why?"

"Because hip and knee replacements both have plastic sockets, which wear down within fifteen to at most twenty years. If I'd had a hip replacement a decade ago, then I would've had to have three or more hip replacements to make it through a normal lifetime." She was weary of explaining this. "And the doctor said a person could really only have it done twice."

"But don't they have metal-on-metal replacements now? One of my department's retirees just had that done last year." After glancing around the room, he sat down on the top of the student's desk opposite her.

"Yes, they can last thirty-five to forty years. But I don't have health insurance." The voices still buzzed in the distance. "And even if I got health insurance, it probably wouldn't cover my preexisting condition."

"Why don't you have health insurance?" His voice resonated with deep concern.

That only intensified her awareness of him. "For the reason I've just named. I'm self-employed, as is my father, and we would have to take out private insurance, which is expensive."

"I didn't realize that."

"It's just a fact of life for many self-employed people." He was so close to her. They were, for once, alone. Awareness of him lapped over her like warm summer waves. "Fortunately, I'm healthy in every other way." She scrambled for another topic.

Ridge did it for her. "I'm trying to do what's best for Ben. I've already told you I was not a good choice of a guardian. His parents evidently didn't have many reliable relatives. But I work in Madison. And Ben is adjusting well here in Winfield—"

"But he's your responsibility, right?"

"Yes, he is my responsibility." Ridge sounded uncertain. Unusual for him.

"You're afraid," she said, feeling her way through this, "he won't want to go back with you after spending the school year and the summer here?"

"Exactly. But how can I fault you and Milo? You've been all that is kind and good."

"I wish I had the answer for you, Ridge," she said softly. She slid off her desk, thinking that they should leave this room with its temptation. Here alone with him, she felt she could say things that she'd felt for many years but had never revealed to anyone. Even to Ridge.

He slid off at the same moment and they came together, face-to-face.

The sudden nearness stunned her into silence. But this silence was rich with emotion and increased consciousness. This was Ridge Matthews, whom she had loved so long ago. She wanted to leave. But she could not move. She could not speak.

And then his hand slowly moved up until it cupped her right cheek.

Now she couldn't breathe. His hand, so large and rough, was touching her so tenderly.

"Why didn't that night change you?" he murmured with wonder in his voice. "My parents are dead except for one fact alone—they're still breathing. But you were there that awful night Dan died. Soon after, you lost your mother. And now you have lost one of your dearest friends, your cousin Ginger. Why aren't you bitter?"

She couldn't find the words. Because with each word he spoke his face had drawn closer and now his lips hovered over hers. She drew in a quarter teaspoon of air but couldn't find room for even that in her lungs.

Then his lips brushed hers once, twice.

She exhaled the tiny breath of air she possessed and moved her lips forward the last fraction. Her upper lip touched his.

"Sylvie…sorry," her father said from the doorway. He shrugged and turned away. "Come on, Ben, we'll just go on to the cafeteria for those cookies."

# SIX

Absolutely and painfully silent in the backseat of Ridge's SUV, Sylvie sat with her hands pressed together and clamped between her knees to hold in her embarrassment. Also in the darkened car, her father sat in front with Ridge. Unaware, Ben fidgeted happily beside her, chatting away with Milo and Ridge about his teacher, his classmates and the cookies in the school cafeteria. After the near kiss she'd shared with Ridge, she was grateful for the darkness on their way home. Her face was warm and she knew she must be glowing bright red.

To Sylvie, enduring those minutes in the cafeteria had been an ordeal. She'd sipped dishwater coffee and munched a dry, tasteless cookie while trying to remain unnoticed. Instead, she'd felt as though a blazing spotlight had been turned toward her and Ridge and everyone had been staring at them. But of course, it had been just her imagination that people were watching her and Ridge.

Finally, Ridge pulled up in front of Milo's. In spite of the chilly darkness, he insisted on accompanying them up to the door. There, with a good-night wave, Sylvie hurried inside and went with Ben to his bedroom. And then on to her own. Her ears had strained to hear what the two men were saying in the other room.

She didn't come out of her bedroom until she had heard the outer door close, signifying Ridge must have left. She sighed at the sound. She could put this behind her now. Crawl into bed and let sleep help her forget.

But her father stopped in her doorway. "Come with me. The Northern Lights are brilliant tonight. Didn't you notice them when we got out of Ridge's car?"

She couldn't decline. So in their darkened apartment, she followed him to the front windows where indeed the Northern Lights—in brilliant neon green with flashes of red—were lilting, dancing above the sleeping giant, the vast ice-ringed Lake Superior. Several minutes of silence passed.

Then her father spoke, "It's good to have Ridge back in Winfield."

She didn't answer, couldn't trust her voice. Had her father been surprised by what happened between her and Ridge tonight? She folded her arms around herself and gazed intently at the natural fireworks before her.

"I'm hoping that Ben can pull Ridge out of the

funk he's been in since that night Dan and you were exploring the lighthouse when you both should have been in bed."

In the past, she had spoken of that night with her father. But she couldn't now, not tonight. Again, she made no comment, biting her lower lip.

"You and Dan were just doing what kids do— taking unthinking, dangerous risks. It was tragic that Dan fell to his death while you fell right beside him but lived."

After carrying a burden of guilt for many years, Sylvie had come to the conclusion that she wasn't responsible for what had happened to Dan. She had allowed God to take away her guilt over her immature argument with Dan—their pushing and shoving—at the top of the old lighthouse. She couldn't have foreseen what the outcome would be or have stopped what happened. After all, she had only been twelve years old, just like Dan.

"I have never understood why Ridge," her father continued in his soothing, rumbly voice, "has always felt that he was responsible in some way for Dan's death. Perhaps because he was the oldest brother. And maybe his parents, not so much in words, but with their attitudes and expressions, blamed him. Just because he was convenient. Not because he carried any real responsibility."

Bringing up Ridge's false guilt finally gave Sylvie something to say. And she found she could draw breath. "Is there anything that we can do to put an end to that?"

"No." Her father's simple negative made her turn and look into his shadowed face.

Would there be no comfort at all for Ridge? "So he will always carry a false guilt?"

"Only God can free us from guilt, both true and false. And only if Ridge will allow God to free him. No words of ours can bring this about. Not the way I see it. We need to ask God to heal Ridge." He put his sinewy arm around her shoulders. "You can love him, Sylvie. But you can't save him." Not giving her a chance to say anything, her father kissed her cheek and then went into his bedroom and quietly shut the door.

For several seconds, she could feel the impression of her father's sweet kiss on her cheek. When Ridge had kissed her, she'd been so embarrassed. But this new attraction growing between them and what others might think of it were secondary to a larger issue. How like her father not to mention the obvious, but to bring up the real, the essence of the matter.

## March 14

The next morning, a lazy snow was falling as Sylvie walked up the steps to her bookshop to begin another day of work. As she unlocked the door, she wondered why she didn't remember pulling down the blind on the entrance door the night before when she closed up. She opened the door. Then she knew *she* hadn't pulled down the shade.

Someone had pulled it down to conceal their breaking into and ransacking her shop. Books, open and closed, lying facedown and faceup, littered the floor of the foyer of the shop. Her desk near the back of the foyer had been pillaged, too.

Shock tingled through her. For long moments, she stood petrified. A scream swelled inside her, but she clamped her lips shut, holding it at bay. She stepped backward and yanked the door shut. With trembling fingers, she punched in the emergency number on her cell phone and told the sheriff's department what she'd found.

Then she sat down on the cold top step and wept. How much more could she—all of them—take?

A few minutes later at the curb in front of Sylvie's bookshop, Ridge slammed on his brakes. He saw her immediately. Sylvie sat on the top step of her shop, crying. The urge to run to her and pull her into his arms nearly overwhelmed him. He shoved open his door. The approaching wail of the sheriff's siren was all that stopped him.

Ridge got out of his vehicle and waited for Keir to join him. It was safer that way. In what he could only describe as a fit of temporary insanity, he had kissed Sylvie only the night before. It wasn't that Sylvie wasn't eminently kissable. Because she was.

But he was leaving Winfield as soon as this case was solved. He'd decided last night that he would let Ben spend part of the summer with Milo. But then he would still send Ben to camp. And in the fall, Ben would go to the boarding school. Winfield was not Ridge's home anymore. And it could not be Ben's. But the troubling question was—how to get this knotty case solved so he could get out of town? And now they faced another crime scene to investigate. He hoped the murderer had left a clue here.

"I was afraid of this!" Keir called to Ridge as he came abreast of him. "I've had deputies patrolling this street every hour since the last break-in."

Ridge pointed to the lowered shade on the front door and to the sun shield lowered inside the large front bay window. "A penlight pointed down wouldn't have shown through that."

Keir hustled up the steps, but Ridge stayed a step behind the sheriff. They halted in front of Sylvie, who was trying to wipe her eyes. Put on a brave front.

Ridge couldn't stop himself. He reached down and helped her to her feet. Her gloved hands trembled within his grasp. She let go as soon as she was steady on her feet. Out of his slacks pocket, he pulled a white handkerchief and handed it to her.

She took it with obvious care, making sure her fingers did not come near his. His gut tightened at her caution. "I'm sorry I broke down like that," she said, his handkerchief muffling her voice, concealing her face, "but it was the shock."

"Finding that a place of our own has been burglarized always comes as a shock," the sheriff said soothingly.

She nodded bravely, still hiding behind the handkerchief.

Ridge felt his face stiffen. *And it sure didn't help if your cousin was murdered a little over a week ago.* That's why Sylvie was crying. Every incident brought back her grief over the loss. Ridge's mood dropped another notch.

"Is the door unlocked?" the sheriff asked.

Before Sylvie could answer him, Deputy Lawson had arrived and come up behind them. "Trish," the sheriff said, turning to her, "I'd like you to drive Sylvie back to her home. And then talk with her briefly about last night when she closed and this morning when she opened up. Then please come back here to work the scene with us. I'll be calling Josh in on it, too."

Ridge experienced conflicting emotions over this crime scene. He was eager to find something the perp had left behind but had the lingering doubt that this scene might also yield no usable clues. But if there were any clue here, he would find it.

"Please," Sylvie spoke up, "I'd like to go to my aunt Shirley's house instead. My dad is gone to

Ashford for the day. Ben's at school. I just don't feel like being alone."

Keir assented to this with a nod. He waved the women away.

Trying to keep his focus on the crime scene, not Sylvie's pain, Ridge followed the sheriff into the foyer and confronted the mess. The sheriff rumbled low in his throat, making his anger audible. Ridge let go a sound of disgust.

"Well, let's get started," Keir declared harshly.

"Yes, let's," Ridge agreed, wishing he could get his hands on the person who had done this. Soon.

After Trish's brief questioning and departure, Sylvie sat at the kitchen table with Aunt Shirley and Rae-Jean. Mugs of cooling coffee sat in front of them, untouched. In an olive-green sweater and slacks, Shirley settled the baby in her infant seat on the kitchen table. The little girl in a pink one-piece sleeper was nearly bald except for a few wisps of strawberry-blond hair.

Shirley slid her index finger under the baby's tiny hand and the baby gripped it. "I'm so sorry for you, Sylvie. All of this is like something that happens on one of those TV crime shows," Shirley murmured. "It doesn't happen to people like us."

Sylvie ached for her aunt. After her mother died, Aunt Shirley had been so good to her. And now Shirley had lost Ginger. And so had Sylvie. And someone was still looking for something. Something so valuable or incriminating that they were willing to tear her shop apart to find it.

Her long blond hair uncombed, Rae-Jean wrapped her arms around herself. Wearing ragged jeans and an old Packers sweatshirt, she looked as if she had endured several sleepless nights. "I wish it would just end. Why can't the sheriff find out who is doing this?"

Neither Sylvie, nor evidently Shirley, had an answer to this. Silence except for Hope's burbling filled the kitchen. "Rae-Jean, how are you feeling?" Sylvie asked, trying to turn the conversation away from the stress of another break-in.

"You don't want to know how I'm feeling," Rae-Jean mumbled, looking away.

"Yes," Aunt Shirley said, "we do want to know how you're feeling."

"Most mornings I wake up wanting to kill myself," Rae-Jean muttered.

Ridge had donned thin plastic gloves. The task before him was a daunting one. Every shelf in the bookstore was empty. Every book had been pulled from the shelf and riffled through.

Keir stood in the doorway to the onetime parlor just off the foyer looking disgusted. "Well, at least we have two more facts to add to our measly total."

Ridge snorted. "I've been so disgusted by this that—pardon me—I haven't come up with even one new fact. Except the obvious, that Sylvie's shop has been torn apart."

Keir held up one finger. "First of all, our murderer-burglar has not yet found what he's looking for."

"Yes," Ridge agreed, "and I suppose you notice that Sylvie's computer has been taken, too." Sylvie's desk at the rear of the foyer had been decimated—drawers pulled out and contents scattered. The computer tower and monitor had been removed.

Keir nodded glumly. "Number two, he's looking for something that could be hidden on a computer or within the pages of a book or behind a book."

"Are we going to have to fingerprint every one of these books?" Just thinking of the task weighed Ridge down.

"If this were just a simple burglary, I probably wouldn't bother with every book. I'd just dust a selection from all the different areas of the shop," Keir replied, glancing around. "But I'm sure you agree that this is connected to Ginger's murder somehow, right?"

"I don't know how we can see it any other way," Ridge grumbled, knowing that they would have to examine each book.

Keir did not say anything more but turned back to the large parlor where he began going through the routine of taking fingerprints. Soon he'd be setting each fingerprinted book back on one of the shelves, too.

Ridge picked his way through the scattered books to the back of the foyer where he'd set up a small collapsible tray-table with fingerprinting materials on it. He bent down and picked up a book to dust it for prints.

The image of Sylvie outside, sitting alone on the top step weeping haunted him. She didn't deserve this. But then neither did Shirley and Tom. Then unbidden came the memory of his lips brushing Sylvie's soft mouth the night before. What had he been thinking of?

Rae-Jean wanted to kill herself? The idea terrified Sylvie. Yet she hadn't been able to come up with a single response to Rae-Jean's dreadful statement. Suicide? Was it that bad?

Shirley rose and went and put her arms around Rae-Jean. "Sweetheart, we didn't know. I thought you'd be happier at home—even with everything that has been going on. What's upsetting you?"

Rae-Jean gasped with what sounded like despair. She bent her head into one hand as though to hide her tears from them. "You have no idea what it's like."

Sylvie rose also and came and stood beside Rae-Jean's chair. "Rae-Jean, tell us. Please."

For several moments, Rae-Jean continued to swallow tears. Finally she looked up and wiped her face with her hands. "I still want to do meth. Every day I have to fight the urge to go back to it."

"I thought you'd gone through withdrawal," Shirley murmured. "Got it out of your system."

"It's not that easy with meth. It's the worst addiction, I think. They told me it actually altered my brain waves. It gives the highest highs, lowest lows."

Sylvie did not know what to say to this.

"What can we do to help you through this?" Shirley asked.

Rae-Jean jumped up. "You are doing everything you can! I shouldn't be laying this on you. You've lost Ginger. And now Sylvie's store has been trashed. I'm being totally selfish."

Ridge continued, picking up book after book, dusting each for fingerprints and then transferring the prints to slides and labeling them. It was tedious, exacting, mind-numbing work. And unfortunately, it left his memory free to go over and over last evening with Sylvie. He recalled her little pearl earrings that had made him want to test the softness of her earlobes. And then he'd kissed her. Why?

No answer came to him except that if given the same circumstances, he would do it again. An unwelcome thought. Also unbidden came the pretty face of Ben's mother on her wedding day. And beside her was his best friend, the groom, and Ridge there as his best man.

Ridge grabbed the next book and dusted it with a vengeance.

\* \* \*

"Rae-Jean, asking others for help," Shirley said, "isn't being selfish." With the knuckles of one hand, she rubbed the back of Rae-Jean's faded green sweatshirt up and down, up and down. "You're right. I am grieving over the loss of my daughter," Shirley admitted. "But your being here with your baby girl gives me a reason to get up every morning. You're helping me go on with my life. And you are here, Rae-Jean, alive. And if you need our help, we will give it."

"Yes," Sylvie agreed, grateful for Aunt Shirley showing her the way. "You're my cousin, too. I love you as much as I loved Ginger. Don't you know that?" She glanced at the baby whose eyes were drifting shut. "And you have this precious little girl. And we love her already, too."

"But I've caused so much pain and suffering," Rae-Jean said, looking up with tear-filled eyes. "Look what I put my little boy and Chaney through when I left them last year. And then I was unfaithful. I think I've must've lost my mind for a while. I don't know how Chaney can even look me in the face without spitting on me."

"Many women," Shirley said in a serious tone and with a gentle hug, "never have a chance to see what their husbands are really made of until the worst happens. I <u>don't</u> recommend it for any marriage. But now you see the kind of man you married very clearly, don't you?"

Rae-Jean nodded, tears pouring from her eyes. "Chaney's been amazing. But how can I ever make it up to him? Little Hope might not even be his baby. Do you know how cheap that makes me feel? I loathe myself."

Long hours passed and Ridge and Keir, along with Josh and Trish, finally took a break and went to lunch at Trina's Good Eats, an institution in Winfield. The original 1927 bell above Trina's door jingled as the three of them entered. They grabbed a booth by the window. Choosing Trina's specialty, a pasty, for lunch, Ridge tried not to growl his order at the blond owner.

"It's all over town that Sylvie's shop got hit last night," Trina said, after taking their orders.

"Then you know all you need to know." Keir looked as if he'd swallowed something sour. "We've been working the crime scene all day."

"When are you going to catch this guy?" Trina persisted.

"As soon as we figure out who it is," Keir said, sounding nettled.

Ridge felt the same aggravation. And more. Was there any way he could speed up this investigation? Was there anything that he was missing? What could Ginger's murderer possibly be looking for? And—a fear that he now recognized and hated to face—how was he going to protect Sylvie?

Sipping his steaming coffee, he put on a calm front. But the truth was he was anything but calm. He clutched his mug and blew on his coffee while it was still much too hot to drink. So far the criminal had been content to merely search *places*. Did the murderer know that Ginger had spent that last evening with Sylvie? The thought sent chills through Ridge. Would Sylvie herself become the next target? How could he stop that?

# SEVEN

*March 16*

On the morning two days after the break-in at Sylvie's shop, Ridge waited in his idling SUV along the curb in front of Sylvie's bookshop. Both agitated and restless, he'd come in hopes of easing her shock when she reentered her store for the first time. After a break-in, people often felt violated. This feeling was intensified when their home or business had also been searched as a crime scene.

But he had another more important reason for coming. He must speak to her alone. *She'll fight me, but this is one argument I'm going to win.*

Then he saw her come around the corner, her head down. She limped across the street, up the walk and steps to her door. Watching her slow progress jabbed him. It wasn't right that most private insurance companies wouldn't insure her because of a preexisting condition. He climbed out of his SUV and hailed her, "Sylvie, wait for me!"

Not appearing nervous at all, she turned and waited for him to reach her. "You didn't have to come this morning, Ridge." She gave him what looked like a forced smile. "I'm all right. My dad offered to come with me, too, today. But I'm all right. Really." Her repetition revealed to him that she was putting up a good front.

"There's something I want to discuss with you." He nodded toward the door and waited while she unlocked it. The two of them walked into the foyer.

Apprehensively he watched as she glanced around. He knew her well enough to expect her reaction to be subtle. After all, she'd barely screamed when she'd seen that Ginger was dead. She wouldn't make a scene today.

"I didn't expect you to put the books back on the shelves," she said, looking around as if everything were new to her.

He wished he could have done more for her.

"That was very thoughtful," she continued. "Having to bend over to gather up all the books would have been hard on me."

This was the first time she'd ever mentioned her damaged hip to him on her own. It gave him courage. He helped her off with her coat and hung it on the hall tree in the foyer.

"Come into the kitchen with me," she invited.

"I'll make coffee." She led him past her ravaged desk and into the kitchen at the rear. She wore a rose cashmere sweater and matching wool slacks, a single pearl pendant at her throat. As usual, well dressed even for a day of putting her plundered shop right again.

"If I ever decided to move out of my dad's place," she said conversationally, "I could easily move in here. I can change the stockroom into a small bedroom. And add a shower to the bath."

He stood in the doorway. The prospect of Sylvie, this lovely and intelligent woman, having to live in such cramped quarters behind her bookshop depressed him. She was too fine, too special to live like that. And this thought gave him the impetus to say what he had come to say. "Sylvie, I want you to take a vacation."

She swung around. "What? What brought that on?"

"I want you to take a vacation now," he repeated. *And I'm not taking no for an answer.*

She stood gazing at him, her hand resting on the kitchen counter. Her large eyes examined his. "Why would you suggest such a thing?"

He made himself stay where he was. "I'm not going to beat around the bush, Sylvie. You're in a very dangerous position."

"Dangerous?" She leaned back against the white-tiled counter and folded her arms in front of herself. "What are you talking about?"

He took one step toward her. She would listen to him. Or else. "Sylvie, you were the last person to see Ginger alive. So far our murderer-burglar has only searched *places*. What if he decides to search...your mind?"

"My mind?" She frowned, one corner of her soft mouth twisted downward.

"Yes, the sheriff and I discussed it last night. When the murderer runs out of places to search, he will come looking for you because you were here to greet Ginger while Tom and Shirley were still in Arizona. You were the one who spent Ginger's last night with her." Ridge took another step nearer, but he held his arms at his sides, elbows locked straight.

"How can you be sure of that?" She glanced away as if he were getting too close to her. Or was he getting too close to the fear she was suppressing?

"The sheriff and I agree that the murderer has so far stayed away from you because he doesn't want any witnesses able to testify against him. But we don't know what he's searching for. He could become desperate, Sylvie. Desperate enough to attack you. And if he does, he won't leave you alive to testify against him."

"But I don't know anything about what he's looking for."

"Yes, and he knows that. Because if you knew what he was looking for, you would have already found it. But you were the person closest to Ginger and you knew things about her that this person doesn't know."

Concentration creasing her forehead, Sylvie gazed at the floor. "You mean he'd think that I knew where Ginger had hidden whatever he's looking for?"

"Exactly." She sounded as if she were going to be sensible about this. Ridge gripped the back of a straight-back chair in the narrow kitchen, still keeping his distance from her. "The sheriff and I think that both you and Milo should take a trip until we have this solved."

Sylvie turned and began to make coffee. "I appreciate your concern. But I can't go on vacation *indefinitely.* Neither can my dad."

He didn't appreciate her dismissal of his concern. "It wouldn't *be* indefinite," Ridge insisted, his tension increasing. He clenched his jaw. "The murderer is bound to give himself away. He can't go on breaking and entering and ransacking without someone seeing him, hearing him, or surprising him in the act. Then we'll nab him."

"Ridge, you know you can't guarantee finding out who's doing this within a certain time frame—"

He tried to interrupt.

She went on talking. "And even if I could afford to get away," she said, not looking in his direction, "I wouldn't leave."

"I knew you would say that—" irritation bit him hard "—but I'm not taking no for an answer. You and Milo are going away until it is safe again for you two here."

"It's not for you to decide, Ridge," she replied, her voice calm on the surface but undergirded with steel. "We couldn't leave Shirley and Tom and Rae-Jean and Chaney at a time like this. And what about Ben? We couldn't leave him alone."

"I'd move into your dad's apartment with Ben." Ridge's hands itched to turn her around to face him. To take him seriously.

"No." Her refusal was serene but firm.

It sparked his temper. Why wouldn't she see sense? He moved up right behind her. "Sylvie, you must—"

"No."

His frustration intensifying with her every word, his reserve melted. He grasped her slender shoulders from behind, his fingers pressing down. "This is a matter of life and death. Your life and death. Perhaps your father's. Or even Ben's because he lives with you."

"I hadn't thought of Ben's safety," she responded. "Perhaps he should move in with someone else—"

Ridge spun her around, his face hot with anger right in front of hers. "Why won't you listen to me?" he demanded.

She moved slightly within his grip, but did not pull away. "It's not a matter for discussion, Ridge. I know you want to protect me. But no one in Winfield is safe until we find Ginger's murderer. No one. Are you going to try to persuade anyone else to leave? Like Shirley and Tom?"

"They don't stand in the personal danger that you do."

She shook her head. "You don't know that."

Her obstinacy snapped the last thread of his restraint. He gripped her delicate shoulders tighter. "I don't want you dead."

She looked up into his eyes. "You're not responsible for me, Ridge. You weren't responsible for Dan, either."

The soft wool of her sweater twisted in his fingers as he tightened his hold on her shoulders again. How could she bring up Dan at a time like this? "This has *nothing* to do with that."

Then he could say no more. He couldn't say, "You're too important to me. I can't lose you, too." He couldn't become attached to anything, anyone who was tied to Winfield. He no longer belonged here. His parents had silently sent him away. If they couldn't have Dan, they wanted no son at all. His long-denied pain manifested itself in a low half groan.

As if it were the most natural thing in the world, she stroked his cheek with her palm—once, twice. "Nothing is going to happen to me, Ridge. You and the sheriff will catch Ginger's murderer."

Her touch had the power to move him. He wished it wasn't so. Her soft, warm palm on his face distracted him from what he'd come to achieve, her safety. Her touch prompted him to think about kissing her lips again. *No.* "What am I going to do with you?" he muttered.

She stared at him, her lovely eyes fringed with golden-brown lashes, gazing at him with such understanding. To her, he was apparently transparent.

Why had he asked her that question? He wasn't going to do anything with her. He just wanted to find the culprit and then escape Winfield for good. But he was weakening.

She stroked his cheek again. Then she stilled. And reminded him of a lovely doe in the forest, becoming aware of another presence. Becoming aware of him.

Had she suddenly sensed how intensely she attracted him? In that moment, he could have forgotten every bit of common sense he owned. And taken her into his arms. And kissed her. As she deserved to be kissed.

Instead she slipped from his grasp. She turned away and finished preparing the pot of coffee. Without looking back, she said softly, "Ridge, I appreciate your concern. But I'm not leaving Winfield. This is my home. There are people here who need me. And I believe you will find whoever has done these awful things. You will find Ginger's murderer."

Afraid to speak, afraid that all the foolish words he must hold back would come spilling out, he turned away and left her there alone.

Back outside on her front step in the cutting

wind, he stared down the side street toward frozen Lake Superior. A few vehicles from Madeleine Island were driving across the thick ice toward town. Though the ice was strong enough at this moment to support a vehicle, it would soon begin melting and cracking, breaking up.

A few moments ago, he'd felt as if he were walking on thinning, quaking ice. And Sylvie's evocative touch had done that to him. His reality, the way he'd chosen to live his life, had felt as if it were breaking up under his feet. Winfield and Sylvie were drawing him home, luring him to dangerously thinning ice. Away from Winfield, his life was simple, easy.

He turned his mind back to the firm ground of facts. There must be another way to persuade Sylvie to leave Winfield until it was safe for her again. He would find the way. And then he'd finish this case and leave. Soon.

In her kitchen, Sylvie stared at the coffee dripping slowly into the glass carafe below. She'd been foolish not to see this coming. But so much had happened over the past weeks. It was like night driving through heavy snow and switching on her bright headlights. The higher beams highlighted the pelting snow and magnified it, so that the road ahead became invisible. One couldn't see anything but the snow falling. Since Ginger's death, she'd been driving with her brights on, snow-blinded by everything that had happened.

Grief over Ginger, worry for her aunt Shirley and Rae-Jean had distracted her from perceiving danger to herself. And the peril was not just to herself but to her heart. Had she really stroked Ridge's cheek just now? She'd definitely miscalculated how much jeopardy he presented to her. She'd thought that she could have him near her yet be able to hide her feelings.

In this moment, Ridge frightened her more than the mysterious killer. Ridge could do more than kill her. He could destroy her. And then walk away. Leaving her breathing but lifeless, crushed.

She couldn't give in to those fears now. Ridge was right. She might become a target. The memory of Ginger's still body froze her to the floor. *Heavenly Father, this is too big, too frightening for me. Should I stay? Or should I go?*

She stared at the calendar. The time was almost up. How long would this take? How many more days? Why had she let herself get sucked into this? It was all getting too creepy. Maxed-out creepy. She couldn't remember trashing the bookshop in town. But she'd been so high that night. Sometimes with Ecstasy, she couldn't remember doing stuff that others told her she'd done. And she did remember throwing books, a lot of books to the floor. But were they the books in that Sylvie's shop? Or were they the books in the dead girl's apartment? Holding her aching head between her hands, she wondered if she was losing her mind. And if she cared. If anyone cared.

That afternoon after closing up shop early, Sylvie stood at the bottom of Shirley's basement steps. On top of everything else today, her clothes dryer had decided to spin its last. So while Shirley was out doing her grocery shopping, Sylvie had lugged her wet clothing over here to dry.

During lunch, Sylvie had almost discussed with her dad Ridge's fears for her. But she'd decided not to. She was afraid that if she had brought up Ridge at all that she might tell her father everything. Tell him how deeply she had begun to care for Ridge once more. Thoughts and feelings had buzzed around in her head till it felt like a busy, teeming beehive.

Standing beside an old, battered table next to the dryer, Sylvie started matching her father's dried socks. She reached to switch on the old radio for distraction. Then she heard the back door just above her open and close. And voices. She froze where she stood.

"Rae-Jean," Chaney insisted, "I don't want to know the outcome of the test."

"But why?" Rae-Jean asked. "It doesn't make any sense."

"I just can't face it right now."

The scraping of wooden chairs being pulled back from the table sounded above Sylvie. Should she let them know that she was here? She felt as if she'd already heard too much. Indecision held her captive.

"I know," Rae-Jean declared, "this is all my fault. We had everything and I went and spoiled it all."

"If you'd been happy, it wouldn't have happened," Chaney replied. "I should have noticed that things weren't right between us. Fact is, I did notice. But I didn't do anything. It's not all your fault."

"Don't try to take the blame." Rae-Jean sounded tearful, fretful. "I was the one who cheated on you. I was the one who was stupid enough to get hooked on drugs."

Sylvie let her hand fall. She was afraid to breathe for fear they'd hear her.

"Elsie Ryerson talked to me about it, Rae-Jean. Elsie made me see that you were vulnerable. I should have protected you, paid more attention. I should have tried to talk to you."

"Elsie is a sweet woman," Rae-Jean said, "but going over how this all happened doesn't help."

"It helped me." Chaney's voice strengthened. "Rae-Jean, you are the only woman I have ever loved. We have a son together. Maybe a daughter. I just can't push you out of my life."

"You can't mean that you think we can get back together," Rae-Jean objected, sounding exhausted, disbelieving. "I'm not strong enough. I don't want you to depend on me. I could go back to drugs at any time. Sometimes I still feel like I did wrong by not giving Hope up to someone who could take better care of her."

Silence. Then Chaney's voice. "You could be stronger than the meth. Don't you believe God can give you the strength?"

"Why would He bother with me," Rae-Jean said, sounding desperate, "and what has that got to do with Hope's paternity test?"

Sylvie heard a chair being pushed back. "God loves you, Rae-Jean. And I don't want to know about the test right now. It's time for me to go. I still have to go next door and say goodbye to our boy then leave for work."

A second chair was pushed back. "Chaney, I don't understand."

"I'll see you soon. I promise."

Sylvie heard Chaney's retreating footsteps, the back door open, frigid air rushing in and down the basement steps. The outside door closed.

She prayed that nothing would bring Rae-Jean down the basement steps. She heard the sound of Rae-Jean walking out of the kitchen. Then from above, Sylvie overheard the creaking of the steps to the second-floor.

Sylvie leaned against one of the beams at the bottom of the basement steps. Guilt warmed her face. *I didn't mean to overhear that, Lord. But what does it mean? Is there anything I can do to help?*

*March 16*

Later that afternoon, Ridge and the sheriff walked toward Milo's shop along the frozen waterfront. Maybe they could make *him* see sense. But Ridge didn't think he'd have success with Milo. Still, they had chosen to visit Milo during school hours so that Ben would be away. As well as during work hours, so Sylvie would be at her shop. As they opened Milo's door, it triggered a small bellows that blew into a duck call, Milo's signature welcome.

In a neat flannel shirt and khaki slacks, Milo looked up from his computer desk behind the glass counter at the rear of the store. His half-glasses perched on his nose. "Just let me finish this e-mail order and I'll be right with you."

Ridge walked along the aisles in the shop, looking at the many lures, sinkers, bobbers and rolls of fishing line. Keir went to the rear aisle and began examining muskie rods. Ridge recalled coming to the shop with his dad when he was just a little kid. The same worn hardwood floor, rough and unpolished, remained underfoot. The walls had never been painted or if they had the paint had worn off many years ago.

Vintage fishing poles and rods were arranged helter-skelter on the walls. Faded photos of fishermen, displaying prize catches, were thumbtacked here and there to the walls. All manner of bait buckets, creels and stringers hung from the ceiling.

In short, it was a store that any fishermen could spend hours in. Happily.

"When was the last time you fished, Ridge?" Milo asked at Ridge's elbow, taking him by surprise.

Ridge stared at Milo. Unable to answer. The peace of the shop had been working its outdoorsy charm on him. He retrieved the reason he had come and put it front and center in his mind. It was too important to let slide.

The sheriff walked toward them. "Did you get in that new muskie rod I ordered for Tom yet?"

"It's still on back order. If I don't get action pretty soon from the supplier, I'll cancel the order and go with the more expensive one."

Keir nodded.

"I'm sorry but I can't believe," Milo said genially, "that you two have come in today to get a jump on the fishing season. What can I do for you?"

"The sheriff and I have been talking," Ridge began, girding himself for battle, "and we both think that you should talk Sylvie into leaving town for a while."

"The idea had already occurred to me." Milo crossed his arms in front of his chest.

Milo's reply startled Ridge. "Then you agree—"

"But I didn't even bother," Milo continued, "to mention it to Sylvie. I knew she wouldn't go for it."

Milo's casual attitude made Ridge grit his teeth. "But your daughter could be in danger, life-and-death danger. You don't want that, do you?"

"It wouldn't be a bad idea for you to leave, too," Keir added.

"How can I leave town? There's Ben to consider. And so many others who need us right now," Milo replied, again aggravatingly calm.

"They are not in as much danger as you are," dge insisted, feeling his blood pressure rise.

"Milo, if others are depending on you, your safety is very important, don't you agree?" Keir said.

Ridge was grateful for Keir's support. How could Milo disagree with that? "And it would be best, safest, if Shirley and Tom went away with you. Couldn't you all go back to Arizona together?" Ridge asked, feeling hope bobbing up inside him.

"Yes, why not?" Keir agreed with enthusiasm in his voice. "This is the slow season. Most shop owners get away now. That's why Shirley and Tom were in Arizona."

"I know you mean well," Milo said, dropping his arms and leaning against the counter of sinkers. "But in a time like this, we need to be here in Winfield where all our family and friends are around us."

Ridge felt his stomach acid begin to burn. "But you must realize that you and Sylvie, especially Sylvie, could be targets? Someone is looking for something that belonged to Ginger. And your daughter was the last person to see Ginger alive. The murderer might decide that Ginger must have told Sylvie wherever it—whatever the thing he's seeking—is hidden. And that for her own reasons, Sylvie hasn't let anyone know she knows about it or has found it. Or that it's something that she hasn't put two and two together about yet."

"All that had occurred to me. But running away wouldn't help, would it? Wouldn't the person ju come after us then? And wouldn't it be easier fo the murderer to get to Sylvie in a place where we are among strangers? We wouldn't even be sensitive to the fact that he is a stranger. Here we can pick out someone who doesn't belong, someone who might hurt Sylvie."

Ridge couldn't think of an answer to that. It was infuriating. Why couldn't he get anyone to listen to reason?

"We can't persuade you, then?" Keir asked, sounding defeated.

"No, and Ridge—" Milo turned his wise light blue eyes on Ridge "—I don't want to be disrespectful or overly personal, but we've chosen a different way. When tragedy strikes our family, we hang together."

The true meaning of Milo's words hit Ridge in the face like a wet oar. The blood drained from his head down to his feet. Milo had just told him, in effect, that Ridge was behaving just like his parents, running, hiding from life. *True or false—that has nothing to do with this.*

Why couldn't he get anyone to understand that this was an extremely risky situation? How could he get them to see that Sylvie was in real jeopardy?

After his abortive interview with Milo, Ridge really had no solid reason to stop and go inside Ollie's convenience store. He didn't need to buy anything there. But he needed to kill time before having to go home to eat supper once more with his silent parents. In his short time here, he'd tightened his belt a notch. The morose silence during each meal made everything his mother cooked taste like shredded newspaper.

And Ollie's store beckoned him because he'd also been thinking that he wanted to see Tanya Hendricks in another setting, away from the sheriff's interrogation room. And it seemed his only other choice was Tanya at work. Her odd behavior and evasiveness that he'd observed while Keir was questioning her had kept niggling him at the back of his mind. Could they be signs of guilt?

He pulled up to one of Ollie's gas pumps and filled his tank, his back to the harsh wind. Then he ambled inside as if he had all the time in the world.

As he wandered through the neat aisles, he watched Tanya out of the corner of his eye. She'd washed up marginally cleaner for work and her royal-blue knit shirt with the little embroidered lighthouse logo looked freshly laundered. He expected her to recognize him, glower at him and watch him hostilely. She didn't. She seemed totally oblivious to him. Was she on drugs at work?

The back door of the convenience store slammed open. Instinctively, Ridge hunkered down between aisles. "Hands up!" a male voice ordered.

Ridge reached inside his coat for his shoulder holster and lifted out the Glock there. He looked up to one of the large moon-shaped mirrors positioned at each corner of the store to frustrate shoplifters. What he saw did not make him happy.

A lean man of medium height with a black snow-mobiling mask pulled over his face was threatening Tanya with a sawed-off shotgun. "Open that cash drawer! Now!" the man shouted, waving the shotgun.

Tanya appeared petrified. She wasn't even blinking.

Ridge didn't make a move. He didn't want to begin shooting up Ollie's convenience store. Especially since he doubted that Tanya would obey his command to drop to the floor. If shots were exchanged, there was a good probability that she would be hit and perhaps killed.

And the masked robber appeared twitchy and nervous. Was the guy on speed? He stuck the barrel of the shotgun right between Tanya's eyebrows. "Open that cash drawer! Now!"

# EIGHT

*No.* Ridge began to rise. Now he had no choice. The robber was going to kill the stunned girl.

Then Tanya snapped into action. She punched buttons, opened the register. She jerked out the cash drawer. And nearly threw it at the robber.

The masked man shoved the cash drawer under his arm. Coins dropped to the floor and rolled. He ran for the back door.

Ridge charged after him. When Ridge burst through the back door, he shouted, "Stop! Police! Stop!"

Oblivious, the robber covered the twenty or so feet of snowplowed asphalt. He then jumped onto a narrow path into the woods behind.

Ridge tore after him. He shot a warning blast into the air. The other man did not even jerk.

Ridge leaped after him into the woods. Someone had forged a deep path through the snow there. "Stop! Police!"

The man didn't even look back.

But Ridge was gaining on him. Closing the gap. He raised his gun again.

Then sharp pain at the back of his head. He felt himself falling.

Ridge heard a voice. Someone was saying his name. He blinked and opened his eyes. Sylvie stood over him; her sweet fragrance filled his head. She held his hand in hers. "Ridge, you can wake up now. Everything is all right."

He blinked again. Groggy. "Sylvie, what happened? Where am I?"

"You're in a room at the hospital in Ashford," she said, her voice gentle and concerned.

He tried to think. Blocked. He tried again. Blocked. "How did I get here?"

"There was a robbery at Ollie's convenience store." With her free hand, she smoothed the pillow beside his face.

Then the robbery, its sights and sounds—that girl's shocked expression, the robber's harsh commands—flooded his mind. "Is that girl…? That Hendricks girl—is she okay?"

Sylvie squeezed his hand. "She's fine. And so are you. You just got a bad bump on the back of your head. And you've been out for a long time."

"What time is it?" He moved his head on the

pillow and yes, he had gotten a bump on his head. It ached like crazy.

"It's nearly seven o'clock. The sheriff, Ben and my dad just went down to get something to eat before the hospital cafeteria closed for the night. I told him I would stay and explain everything to you if you woke up while he was gone."

Ridge lifted his head briefly. The room swirled in front of his eyes. He groaned silently and laid his head back on the pillow.

"Do you remember what happened to you?" she asked, again smoothing his pillow, her soft hand grazing his face.

He struggled to remember, clamping his eyes shut, trying to pull up the images that must lie buried in his memory. Finally he began to see them. "I was chasing the robber. I was behind Ollie's store and...someone hit me from behind."

"That's what Tanya Hendricks said happened. She said you must have been hit from behind. She found you on the path, facedown, bleeding from the back of the head. She was the one who called the police."

Ridge squirmed on the bed, preparing to try again to lift his splitting head from the pillow. Because somehow it was imperative that he face this situation sitting up.

Sylvie pressed his shoulder down. "Don't get up yet. The doctor said that would only make the headache worse."

"Well, that's what he says," Ridge complained. "Frankly I think I would be better if I sat up and didn't put pressure on the bump. It hurts like the blazes."

She chuckled softly and reached for his bed control handset. "Okay, why don't we use the controls? We'll let power raise your head." Slowly the head of his bed rose until he was almost sitting up. "Is that better?"

He began to nod yes and stopped himself, grimacing with another acute twinge of pain. He hated to be so helpless in front of Sylvie. He felt his neck and face flaming with embarrassment. He avoided Sylvie's eyes.

The nurse bustled in and took his vitals, handed him pills in a little paper cup and told him to swallow them. She hurried out.


"My father called your parents about your injury." Sylvie looked away. Seeing Ridge in a hospital bed had shaken her. And he looked embarrassed to be caught by her in this weakened state. She hadn't considered that particular reaction from him. *I should have.* But all she'd wanted to do was be with him, to be reassured that he was really all right.

She fought the urge to touch him again, hold his hand in hers. She made herself turn away and sit down in the bedside chair. "Your parents were glad to hear that you weren't seriously hurt. They didn't come since you would be released in the morning anyway. And you would be home tomorrow." Sylvie couldn't imagine her father behaving like this if she'd just been the one attacked.

"I've been knocked unconscious before. Not often. But a few times. In my line of work, it happens. They've gotten used to it."

Sylvie hadn't thought of this before. Maybe part of the reason Ridge's parents shut him out wasn't just losing Dan. Maybe Ridge's being in law enforcement made them fearful. Fearful of losing their only remaining son.

"Did they get him?" Ridge asked, interrupting her thoughts. "Did they get the guy with the sawed-off shotgun?"

"No, they didn't. But you're fine." She realized then that she was still tense. Too many dangerous events, too close for comfort. "And Tanya was unharmed. That's what's important, right?"

Ridge did not look as if he agreed though he shrugged slightly.

Ben and her dad appeared at the doorway. "He's awake!" Ben ran to Ridge, but halted a step from his bedside.

Sylvie said a quick prayer. *Ridge, please offer your hand to Ben.*

Whether by divine intervention or by instinct, Ridge did offer his hand to his ward. "Don't worry about me, Ben. I'm pretty tough."

Ben took Ridge's hand briefly. Relief was etched

over his young face. Sometimes Sylvie forgot that it had been less than a year since this young boy had lost his parents. She was grateful when her father walked over to stand behind Ben. He put both his hands on Ben's shoulders. It was a comforting but very masculine gesture. She wondered suddenly if her father had ever wanted a son.

"I've been telling Ben you're tough," Milo agreed. "I told him you'd probably be ready to go ice-fishing with us in a couple of days."

"Sounds like fun," Ridge said, but without any real evidence of pleasure.

Sylvie hid a grin. To her dad, a good day fishing fixed everything.

"Keir went home," Milo said. "He said you should come in to the department when you feel up to it. He said something about an FBI agent coming tomorrow."

"FBI?" Ridge repeated.

Milo smiled. "That should perk you up. A date with the FBI is just what you needed to get you back in gear."

But the mention of the FBI tightened all Sylvie's muscles. So the FBI had checked out ELF. What would the FBI have to say about Ginger's assistant professor's theories about ecoterrorists?

Sylvie rose, hoping her tense reaction didn't show. "We should be leaving you, then. They told us you need your rest."

Ridge looked disgruntled. In farewell, Ben and her dad in turn gripped Ridge's hand.

Resisting the urge to kiss Ridge goodbye on the cheek, she smoothed his blanket. Then she waved and followed Ben and Milo from the room. *Ridge, leave Winfield soon. My resistance to loving you and letting it show is nearly spent.*

But maybe the FBI visit would allow Ridge to go back to Madison. Conflicting emotions struggled within her. *I want Ridge to stay. I want him to go.*

*March 17*

The next morning, Ridge approached Sylvie's bookshop from the rear. His head still ached. But he'd felt worse. After leaving the hospital, he'd stopped by the Sheriff's Department. There he'd been told that the sheriff had gone to Ginger's apartment with the FBI agent sent to investigate any connection between Ginger's murder and ecoterrorism.

Ridge wanted to speak to the FBI agent face-to-face. Then he'd get a feel about whether he should trust what the agent had to say and he was curious about what the FBI might have uncovered. He hoped it would be substance not just steam. Experience had taught him long ago it only took one good break to solve a case. That's all it usually ever took, but it could be so frustrating waiting for that one slipup by the perpetrator. Or a valid witness would give one clue; something they finally remembered seeing or hearing or knowing would surface in their consciousness. And like someone whisking off a mask, this fact would reveal the perpetrator. Had someone in Winfield forgotten something crucially important?

With cautious steps, he let himself in the back door where just two weeks ago Sylvie and Ben had found Ginger's lifeless body. For the first time, he wondered if it bothered Sylvie to work so close to the place where she and her family had suffered such a loss. He pushed these thoughts aside and trudged up the steps. Just inside Ginger's apartment, he found Keir and a stranger, dressed in a gray trench coat over a dark suit.

The introductions were accomplished quickly. The FBI agent, Kinkade, got right down to facts. "I don't think that Miss Johnson's murder is connected to any of the ecoterrorists in my jurisdiction."

"Then there are some in northern Wisconsin?" Ridge asked, feeling vindicated.

"Yes, unfortunately. South of here near Crandon, a mining company has been trying to start up new lead mining operations for the past few years. The law-abiding environmentalists have been vigorously campaigning against this. But unfortunately, it has attracted some crazies and they've damaged some property. And sent some threatening letters to various mining officials and townspeople who were in favor of the new mine."

"But Kinkade says that none of them have any history of violence or any connection with any group from the Northwest," Keir added.

Hearing the sound of steps on the staircase, Ridge hoped it wasn't Sylvie coming up. And he wasn't completely convinced that the FBI agent had it together. But he wasn't going to try to persuade Kinkade. What he wanted now was some more information. "Do you know, Kinkade, of any extreme militants in this area?"

"None." Kinkade's tone held no doubt.

Then Sylvie appeared at the door of Ginger's apartment. Keir waved her in.

"I heard voices." She looked drawn and paler than usual.

The memory of her gentle touch last night curled through him. A desire to protect her swept through him like wildfire. Concerned about her and about this reaction, he watched her face but held his hands at his sides.

"I'm so glad to see you up and about, Ridge," she said, glancing at him.

Grinning, Kinkade stepped forward, hand outstretched. "I'm Vince Kinkade."

Keir performed the introductions.

Ridge noted the way the man was looking at Sylvie, who was attractively dressed as always. She was a striking woman.

To Ridge's relief, the sheriff thanked Kinkade

for coming. That didn't leave Kinkade any choice but to leave.

And Ridge listened to the man return down the steps and a few minutes later to the sound of his SUV driving away.

"I'll be going back to my shop, then," Sylvie said, turning to go down the steps.

With effort Ridge stood where he was and let her go. Compelling memories of her soft hand holding his last night taunted him.

Keir studied Ridge. "Do you have any idea who it might have been robbing Ollie's store yesterday or who gave you that blow on the head?"

It took a moment for Ridge to switch gears. His head still ached. "I've been thinking about that. I don't think it can have anything to do with Ginger's death. But I think I know who might have done it."

*March 19*

It was Saturday afternoon. Sylvie found herself at the Matthewses' back door. Standing there took her back to the days when she used to come knocking to rouse Dan to come out and ride bikes, a bittersweet memory. But she had a question she must ask Ridge and it had drawn her here irresistibly.

She shivered in the cold. But beside the door, a welcome purple crocus peeped out from the snow. The door opened and she was face-to-face with

Ridge's mother. "Hello," Sylvie said with a smile. "Is Ridge around?"

"Ridge!" The woman called over her shoulder but did not return Sylvie's smile; she merely stepped back to allow Sylvie to enter. Then after a brief greeting and offering condolences over the loss of Ginger, she left the immaculate room.

Mrs. Matthews always treated Sylvie that way. Sylvie tried not to take it personally. But she was grateful to see Ridge come into the kitchen.

"Has something happened?" Ridge asked.

She didn't blame him. Only a murder and burglaries linked them. Otherwise, he would be in Madison now. "No, but I just wondered if you would like to take a drive…or something." *Then we can be alone and talk.* Of course, that was the last thing she should want but she had to ask Ridge, right?

"Sure." Ridge reached for his overcoat and ushered Sylvie out of his parents' house as if he realized how uncomfortable it was for her and for his parents to have her there.

From his seat by the bar's smudged window, he looked down the empty street toward Milo's Bait and Tackle Shop. He'd been here, down the waterfront from Milo's, watching, waiting and hoping for a chance. The chance had come. The old man and the kid had schlepped out to ice-fish in the old guy's shack. Then he'd seen that pretty blonde come out and walk away. So the apartment was empty.

He swallowed the rest of his stale beer, got up and walked outside into the brisk wind. Should he enter by the rear or by the front—the question he'd mulled over had finally been decided. From the alley, he walked onto the shoveled path to the rear entrance of the shop. And mounted the stairs to the apartment. He slid the glass cutter out of his pocket. After his first "visit," he couldn't count on their continuing their usual practice of not locking the doors. So he figured it wouldn't be as easy this time. He'd come prepared.

Ridge drove Sylvie along the shore of frozen Superior, heading back toward Milo's shop. He'd wanted to see Sylvie today and had been fighting the temptation to seek her out.

He'd even told Milo he wasn't up to ice-fishing yet, giving his recent head injury as an excuse for not joining Milo and Ben. And all for nothing. Here he was with Sylvie anyway. "What is it you wanted to discuss?" he asked.

"I was curious about why that FBI agent was in town. I've heard all kinds of odd theories—from a bank robbery south of here, to the robbery at Ollie's."

"They're all wrong." Gossip annoyed him as usual, but he kept that from his voice. Sylvie sitting so near was temptation. Why was it increasingly difficult to ignore her as he had in the past? *You never ignored her,* his conscience taunted him. *You just always left town fast.*

Ridge gripped the wheel with both hands and cleared his throat. "Kinkade was here to let us know that he doesn't think terrorists could have anything to do with what happened to Ginger."

She nodded. "I was afraid of that. It's been a little over two weeks since her murder. Have you made any progress?" She bent her elbow and leaned on the door, and rested her forehead on the window, looking as if her head pained her. "Is there any hope?"

He finished cutting a four-inch square out of the window on the outside door. He tapped the square and the glass fell inside, shattering with a soft tinkling sound. His thick sweatshirt sleeve protecting his wrist, he reached inside and felt for the doorknob. Found it, turned it and let himself in. So far so good.

He stood in the quiet apartment, listening for any sound that would alert him that he might not be alone. Last time he'd thought it was empty but he'd had to knock out that pretty blonde. Nothing. He quickly opened, rifled and slammed kitchen drawers. Nothing. He flung open kitchen cabinets feeling around the bottom of each one for any kind of bulge or concealment. Nothing. He cursed.

In the living room he began pulling down books and magazines, tossing them helter-skelter. There wasn't any other place it could be. It had to be here. *I have to find it before it's too late.*

Ridge didn't appreciate Sylvie's question about progress on the case. But he recognized his annoyance resulted from the fact he and the sheriff hadn't made any headway. Someone was looking for something that evidently they were willing to kill for. He still didn't know what it was. Was the FBI agent correct? Or was there something to do with Ginger's research that someone wanted to stop and the FBI had missed it?

"Sorry," she apologized, touching his sleeve. "I know I shouldn't ask you. It's all so frustrating. And I'm sure you're the most frustrated of us all. You wanted to take Ben to that school. And now you just want to get home to Madison, don't you?"

When he heard her final question, something happened that Ridge hadn't expected. Suddenly he felt that of all the places in the world he could be right now, he was right where he wanted to be. Sitting here next to Sylvie Patterson. The realization made it impossible for him to speak for a few moments.

And made him regret that he'd chosen to drive her directly home instead of taking a more circuitous route.

* * *

He heard footsteps coming up and cursed silently. Only one exit. He had to go through the door he'd come in. From under his thick sweatshirt, he dragged out the snowmobiling mask and pulled it on. He ran straight to the one door and out. The old man and the kid were halfway up the steps. He barreled down the stairs right at them. He knocked the old guy into the kid. They fell back and sprawled on the steps. He leaped over them. As he hit the sidewalk he stumbled, got back on his feet and raced for the alleyway. He heard the shout, "Stop, thief!" *Yeah, right.*

Ridge heard the shout. Milo was sprawled at the foot of the stairs to the apartment. Ben, jumping up and down, waved to Ridge from Milo's side. Ridge slowed and pressed the electric switch that lowered the window.

"That guy was in our apartment!" Milo bellowed.

"The guy wearing the snowmobiling mask!" Ben shrieked, pointing toward the alley. "He just went that way!"

At the mention of a snowmobiling mask, Ridge pressed the accelerator all the way to the floor. Was this the same guy who'd robbed Ollie's? At the corner, Ridge careened toward the alleyway. A man in a snowmobiling mask slipped between houses. Ridge gunned the motor again and they careened around the next corner to cut him off.

But the guy never emerged on the next street.

Ridge backtracked. He drove up and down the nearest alleys and streets. Finally, watching the area intently, he slowed and pulled out his cell phone. He punched his speed dial and told the sheriff what had happened, leaving the details of the APB and the house-to-house search up to Sheriff Harding.

Then Ridge caught sight of Deputy Josh on patrol and flashed his lights to wave him down. Josh pulled alongside. As Ridge was filling him in, Josh's radio came to life, ordering all deputies to the waterfront for a house-to-house search.

"I'm going to walk home." Sylvie started to get out.

"No!" Ridge ordered. "You could be the one the suspect is looking for."

She frowned but didn't argue.

Then Keir Harding roared up behind Ridge. And another deputy. Keir got busy instructing his deputies on how to proceed.

"Ridge," Sylvie pleaded, "my father may be hurt."

Keir nodded and asked Ridge to take her home and protect Milo's place, the crime scene.

Ridge felt he was their best eyewitness but reluctantly drove back to Milo's Bait and Tackle Shop. "Your apartment is a crime scene now. We'll just go and get your dad and Ben and make sure they are okay."

With her at his side, Ridge climbed the steps to Milo's apartment. He found Milo and Ben at the kitchen table. Ben was holding a wet dishcloth against the back of Milo's head. "Ridge, he's hurt. He hit his head," Ben said.

Sylvie hurried to her father's side.

"Milo," Ridge asked, "how bad are you?"

"It's not just my head," Milo admitted. "I think I may have broken some ribs and I banged up my knee pretty good. I had trouble walking up here. Ben had to help me. I don't think I can walk."

Ridge sank into the kitchen chair opposite Milo and called dispatch again to request medical assistance. Dispatch told him that Keir had already put in a call to Ashford Hospital. When Ridge hung up, he looked around at the disaster area which now comprised Milo's apartment. "Did you get a good look at him?"

Ben answered, "He was wearing that snowmobile mask and was wearing dark clothing. That's all I saw."

"Me, too," Milo muttered. "It all happened so fast. We were just walking up the steps…" The older man's voice faltered.

"That's what happened," Ben put in. "We were just walking up the steps and he ran right at us. He knocked us clear off our feet. And then he ran away. We wanted to follow him, but Milo's knee hurt him and I didn't want to leave him."

Ridge welcomed the noise of an ambulance siren in the distance. Getting Milo help, as well as Ben and Sylvie somewhere safe, was a priority. It would also free him up to get back to the hunt.

* * *

Hours later, Ridge was finally able to enter Milo's hospital room. Had it just been a couple of days since he was here as a patient?

When he glanced at the bed, he found Milo, lying with his eyes closed. And on the bed beside Milo, curled up like a puppy, was Ben. Sitting in the chair by the bed, Sylvie opened her eyes and looked to Ridge. "How are you?" she asked in her soft voice.

Her genuine concern for him wrapped around his heart, warm and comforting. How like her to think of others before herself. "I'm fine. Just irritated that I can't catch this guy. I can't believe he had the nerve to break into your apartment in broad daylight."

"It does speak of desperation. I wonder what he's looking for." She shook her head and grimaced as though annoyed with herself. She gave a half laugh. "Of course, if we knew that, there would be no more questions."

He shrugged.

Welcoming the opportunity for a break, Sylvie stood. Ridge looked as though he needed one, too. "Let's step outside for a few minutes. I need some fresh air. They'll be fine here." She smiled at the bed.

He walked beside her down the hall, into the elevator and then out through the emergency entrance. Tonight, a breath of spring was in the air, softening it and bringing the hope of daffodils and tulips. She breathed again deeply. Gratefully.

"Did they find out anything about the man who broke into our apartment?"

He shook his head.

She led him down the walk toward the city street and finally voiced what she was thinking though it pained her. "You still want to leave, don't you? Can't you persuade your boss that this is a lost cause?"

"You know why I'm staying. There's a murderer still at large here. You're still at risk."

She paused beside a cement retaining wall. She leaned against it, folded her arms, crossed her ankles and gazed into his eyes. "You can't protect me day and night. You know that, right?"

He ignored her comment. "How is Ben taking all this?"

"Ben is fine. Or will be. They're just keeping my father overnight for observation. I'll pick him up in the morning."

"Good. Sylvie, I want you to take me seriously—"

The sheriff's Jeep roared up the lane to the emergency room. Keir slammed on his brakes, got out and walked over to them. "How are you doing, Sylvie? How's Milo?"

She smiled and nodded. "We'll mend." She hoped he didn't see her lower lip tremble.

"Have you found anything new?" Ridge demanded.

Keir pulled his lips back in a silent snarl. "Not much. But we haven't given up. Sylvie, I'm afraid you won't be able to go home tonight. I have a deputy going over every millimeter of your apartment. That's going to take all night. And probably most of tomorrow."

This was not welcome news to her. But she had expected it. Crime scenes were becoming a part of her life—unfortunately.

"Have you found anything new?" Ridge repeated.

Keir grimaced.

"I think I should go back inside," Sylvie said, suspecting that they would like to speak alone. She started to move away.

"Just a moment, Sylvie. I know I've asked you this before, but can't you think of any hiding place in your apartment?"

"Sheriff, after the first time someone broke in and attacked Rae-Jean while she was staying with us, my dad and I went over and over this. We couldn't think of anyplace or anything."

Keir spread his arms wide. "That's what I thought you'd say."

Ridge and the sheriff watched Sylvie reenter the emergency room entrance. Then Ridge demanded, "Okay, what have you got?"

"The intruder shed his mask. Trish found it tossed under someone's front steps only a block from Milo's. Or we think it must be the intruder's mask. It matched the description that you and Milo gave of the one you saw. And no one in the house where it was found or the surrounding neighbors claimed it as theirs."

"So he shed the mask and became just somebody in town. Not our fleeing suspect."

Keir nodded grimly, his arms folded high and tight. "You told me that you thought it might have been Doyle Keski who robbed Ollie's convenience store."

Ridge nodded, feeling as grim as Keir looked.

"Do you think this was Doyle Keski?"

"It's hard to say. But I think this man was taller and had a larger build than Keski has. And the guy in the convenience store robbery wore a knit ski mask and the guy today was wearing a snowmobiling mask."

"Yeah," the sheriff agreed, "you're right. This guy was wearing a snowmobiling mask that just covers the front of the face with a band around the back so it will fit under a snowmobiling helmet."

"Right, I mean, it's not like he couldn't own both a knit ski mask and a snowmobiling mask, but why would he use different face coverings for different crimes?"

The sheriff shrugged. "I'm going home. I'll have a full day tomorrow going over everything that Trish finds tonight. I don't know if I'll be able to shut my brain off and sleep. But I'm going to try."

"I'm going back in. I need to take Sylvie to Shirley and Tom's. When Sylvie called to tell them that Milo was in the hospital, they invited Sylvie and Ben to spend the night with them."

The sheriff turned away. "Good." Soon after a weary wave, he drove away.

Ridge stared up into the darkening sky. *God, please cut us some slack. Just one break. That's all we need to get this guy.*

Ridge walked back into the hospital, wishing he was as confident as Sylvie about God's loving care. Upstairs, he helped Sylvie into her coat. Milo said Ben wanted to sleep on a cot beside Milo's bed instead of leaving. Ridge agreed and parked his car in the alley behind Shirley and Tom's house. Sylvie surprised him by sending Ben ahead into the house.

"Ridge, you've been wanting me to go away. And I have resisted you. Because it just doesn't feel right to leave my family at this time. But perhaps I am endangering my father and Ben."

These were welcome words. "I'm glad you're finally seeing sense—"

"I think I should move into the apartment above my shop. Then I wouldn't endanger anyone else."

Ridge slapped the steering wheel once. "Over my dead body. That would be like baiting a trap."

"I hadn't thought of it like that. Maybe that's just what we should do."

Not wishing to be rude, Ridge made no response.

He got out of the vehicle and went around and opened the door for Sylvie.

She looked up at him in the low light radiating from the back of Shirley's house. "Ridge, you may not like it, but my moving to Ginger's apartment might flush out her murderer."

He leaned close to her face and declared, "I don't want to hear another word about this."

Sylvie stood up and Ridge did not step back. They were face-to-face, nose-to-nose. "I'm going to suggest it to the sheriff."

"He will never agree to such a thing."

"We'll see about that."

# NINE

Sylvie stared at Ridge, her jaw set. Why couldn't
he see that this made perfect sense? "I thought you
wanted to get back to Madison."

"Do you think I want to get back to my regular
job at the expense of your safety, possibly your life?"

She'd exhaled loudly in disgust. "This can't go
on unresolved. Something has to be done."

"I don't believe you. We just left your father at
the hospital with broken ribs. Didn't that teach
you anything?"

His undeniable concern flowed through her like
July sunshine. But she couldn't let that sway her.
"We can't go on like this. The tension is getting to
all of us. And there was too much going on already."

"What do you mean by that?"

They were so close that his warm breath fanned
against her cheek. "I mean that Tom and Shirley lost
Ginger. I mean that Chaney and Rae-Jean have to
decide what to do about their marriage. I mean Ben

is just now getting settled with us. And you want to take him away." Reciting the litany of all the things that hurt her family this month hit her afresh. Embarrassing tears filled her eyes. She turned her head away quickly so he wouldn't see them.

His strong hands gripped her shoulders once again. "You need to listen to me. You don't know murderers. I do."

Facing him again, she leaned her head against his broad, reassuring shoulder. "Ridge, I'm just so tired. I want to end this. I'm willing to do *anything* to make that happen." Her agitation drained away; all she wanted was to stand here close to Ridge. Here she was safe. But that was an illusion.

He made a hissing sound of disapproval. "Let's get you inside. You're dead on your feet." He pulled her forward, shut and locked the car door behind her.

Sylvie let him lead her up the back walk with his hand under her elbow. Her head ached. Her hip ached. She felt a little dizzy.

At the top of the back steps, Shirley threw the door wide-open. "We've been waiting for you. How is Milo?"

"He'll be home tomorrow." Sylvie let Ridge help her up the steps into the warm, bright kitchen.

Though she longed for Ridge's embrace, she went right into her aunt Shirley's arms.

"Are you sure Milo's all right?" Shirley asked again, holding Sylvie close. Aunt Shirley's fragrance, lily of the valley, further calmed Sylvie, filled her with memories of protection.

Ridge answered for her, "He'll be released tomorrow. Shirley, Sylvie is exhausted."

Shirley said nothing but took Sylvie's hand and led her toward the hallway.

Sylvie halted, looking back at Ridge, taking in the way he watched her with such concern. But she couldn't give in. "I am going to talk to the sheriff about my idea. He might have a different opinion than yours."

Ridge frowned at her and waved a hand. "Go to sleep. We'll talk in the morning."

Looking at him was risky. He'd claimed some of her heart again. So after one last reluctant glance at Ridge, Sylvie followed Shirley into the hallway.

Ridge stepped closer to Tom and in an undertone said, "I'm going to sleep on your sofa tonight."

Tom gazed at him. "Do you think that's necessary?"

Ridge nodded, his lips tight. "I wish it weren't."

"You and me both." Tom turned and over his shoulder, motioned Ridge to follow him. In the dimly lit living room, Tom waved Ridge to the sofa. "I'd give you a bed if we had one left. I'll go get you a pillow."

Tom delivered the pillow and a blanket and left Ridge alone. Divested of his outercoat, Ridge stood in the darkened living room alone. He listened to the sounds of the house and neighborhood. A dog barking in the distance. The creaking of the old floor as someone moved overhead. The loud ticking of the mantel clock. Nothing could have been more peaceful than this setting.

He unhooked his shoulder holster and took it off. Following routine, he checked his gun. Then he slipped the Glock underneath the pillow where he could reach it within seconds. Sitting down on the couch, he unlaced his shoes and slipped them off. After stretching his arms overhead, loosening his tense neck and shoulders and gently probing the tender spot on the back of his head, he lay down and stared up at the ceiling.

Just like this quiet home, Winfield was deceptively peaceful tonight. But evil prowled in the shadows. He had to come up with some way to protect Sylvie. From the murderer. From her own reckless idea.

Several miles away at Bugsy's, the barkeep, Joe Novinsky, locked the last customer out. If it had been a hot summer night, he would have stayed open until 2:00 a.m. But in the late winter, he usually closed up well before midnight. He shuffled back toward the bar to wash up the last few glasses. He'd clean up the rest in the morning.

Just before he went behind the bar again, he heard movement behind him. He swung around.

Some guy with a knit ski mask over his face was pointing a sawed-off shotgun at Joe's chest. In forty years of bartending, Joe had only been in this situation twice before. He hadn't wanted to make it three. Especially, he hoped, not if three strikes meant he would be out.

"Open the cash register!" the robber shouted in the quiet room. "Move it. Move it."

Joe didn't argue. His life was worth more than the lousy till. He pushed a key and the cash register drawer popped open.

"Put it in this!" The robber shoved a paper bag at Joe.

Joe quickly emptied the till into the bag and handed it over.

"Get down on the floor! Facedown! Put your hands behind your neck! Stay that way!"

Joe obeyed and then heard the sound of footsteps running away. He felt the rush of cold air when the door opened and closed. He lay there for several more minutes listening to the sound of a rough motor roaring to life and then racing away at high speed.

Finally, he pushed himself up onto his knees, grabbed the seat of a nearby chair and pushed himself up straight. His old bones sure ached tonight. He cursed quietly. After looking outside, he walked over to the telephone and dialed 911. How dumb could the guy with the gun be? The answer was painfully obvious.

\* \* \*

Ridge blinked his eyes. He rubbed them with the heels of his hands. Then he heard it again. His cell phone was ringing. He pulled it off the coffee table and flipped it open. He glanced at the luminous dial of his watch. It was nearly twelve-thirty at night.

"Sorry to bother you so late," the sheriff apologized. "But there's been a holdup at Bugsy's. It might be the guy who robbed Ollie's convenience store."

"Did you nab him?" Ridge swallowed a yawn.

"No, but the barkeep says he thinks he knows who it is. Do you want to come with me to question the barkeep and maybe pick up the suspect?"

Ridge hesitated, again fighting the deceptive peace of this place. "I'm sleeping at Tom and Shirley's house. If I come out to you, would you have a deputy come and sit outside in the alley behind Shirley's while I'm gone?"

"No problem. See you there." The sheriff hung up.

When Ridge arrived, the sheriff's Jeep was already parked beside Bugsy's door. Yawning, Ridge got out and let himself into the tavern. The sheriff and an older guy with a bald head and gray stubble on his chin sat at one of the small tables. Ridge wondered if this was a worthless trip or if this might connect with Ginger's murder. But then most of police work was comprised of worthless trips, endless questions and general frustration.

The sheriff greeted Ridge laconically. "Joe here says he thinks he knows who the robber is."

"Yeah—" Joe nodded at Ridge "—the guy could star on the *Stupid Thieves* show. Or is it *Stupid Criminals*—that special they do sometimes on TV."

Ridge slumped into the chair between the two men. "Let me guess. Doyle Keski."

"Not bad," the older guy said.

"How did you come up with that one?" Keir asked, sounding impressed.

Ridge shrugged. "We went to high school together. Doyle hasn't changed much. Did you see his face?"

"No, he was wearing a ski mask."

Ridge sat up straighter. "A ski mask or a snow-mobile mask?"

"A ski mask—a knitted hat with holes for eyes and mouth. Not a snowmobile mask with a strap around the head that fits under the helmet." Joe showed the difference with his hands.

Interesting. Was this two men or one man with two kinds of masks? "Okay. Go on."

"Doyle was in here tonight drinking," the old guy said with a half smile. "He must have gone into the bathroom right before closing and just stayed in there. In the summer tourist season, I usually check the restrooms before shutting down for the night. But not in the winter months with just locals. I mean, the snowmobiling season is even over. It's been dead around here."

Ridge wished the guy would get to the point. So far none of this had anything to do with the case he'd stayed in Winfield to solve.

"Anyway, when I locked the door tonight," Joe continued, "I noticed that old rust bucket Keski calls a truck was out in the parking lot. And after the robber left and I got up, I looked out and the truck was gone. Unbelievable." The older guy shook his head.

That sounded to Ridge like the kind of thing the teenage Keski, whom he recalled from high school, would've done. Obviously, he hadn't expanded brainwise since he left high school.

The sheriff promised to follow up and Joe said he would just close up and go home. He was too tired to do anything else. A few moments of fright had tired him out and he'd already been dragging. Ridge and Keir left together.

"I'm sorry I bothered you," Keir said. "I thought it might be connected to the robbery at Ollie's convenience store or to the more serious crime that we're investigating."

"You might be right on one. Keski might be the one who held up Tanya at Ollie's," Ridge said, standing by his car.

"You don't think he might be the one who knocked Milo down the stairs today?"

"Well, you have the snowmobiling mask. After a DNA test, that might provide your answer." Ridge pulled up his collar against the chill. "But the bartender said that this guy was wearing a ski mask, not a snowmobiling mask. But we don't know if that is even helpful."

"Yeah. Going to pick up Keski feels like fishing in a bucket." Keir waved and got into his Jeep. "You can head back to Shirley's. I'll get a deputy to go with me to pick up Keski." He slammed his door.

Ridge didn't argue. He waved goodbye and got into his SUV. He needed his sleep tonight because tomorrow he had to reason with Sylvie.

He was slumped in his favorite chair and he heard someone pounding on his door. His heart skipped a beat. Had the sheriff somehow connected him to the attack on Milo Patterson or the robbery? Or was it them, coming to pressure him again? He shook himself and stood up. He was getting paranoid. It might just be a late customer. He trudged to the door and opened it a crack. And he didn't like who he thought he saw outside. "What do you want?"

"It's me. Open up." He recognized her voice.

He didn't want her around, complicating things any more than they were. "Go away. I don't have anything for you." He started to shut the door.

She pushed against it, halting him. "You owe me. You owe me big-time. You give me what I want or I'm going to go straight to the sheriff."

He threw open the door. And glared at her. "You're becoming a real pest."

"And you're a jerk. We all got problems." She wavered on her feet. She looked a mess. "Now give me what I want. I've got to have it."

He turned away from the door, slamming it behind him. He heard her pounding on the door again. He took his time getting out what she wanted. He sauntered back to the door and enjoyed listening to her pound and yell for him for a few more moments.

Then he opened the door and threw the bag into her face. "Here. Don't come back again. Your credit isn't good here anymore."

He slammed the door in her face. But the satisfaction was momentary. Time was running out. He had to find it, He had to get the money. Or make a run for it. Or he'd be dead.

*March 20*

Ridge sauntered into the sheriff's neat office the next morning. He was confident that Keir would agree with him even if he had to persuade him. But he would hold back at first. He didn't want to let it show how much Sylvie's idea bothered him. The suspicion that the sheriff might agree with Sylvie sharpened the edge to Ridge's voice. "So how did everything go with arresting Keski last night?"

"No problem. But we didn't find the money on him." Keir waved Ridge to the chair on the other side of his desk.

"Were you able to arrest him?" Ridge sat down and shrugged out of his overcoat.

"I'm going to talk to the county prosecutor. If nothing else, I think I can get a court order to insist that Keski give us a DNA sample."

"You're going to try to tie him to the snowmobile mask found after the break-in at the Pattersons'?" Ridge shifted in his chair, fighting the tension that seized him.

The sheriff nodded.

Unexpectedly, Ridge's mind brought up a parade of images: Ginger's body lying twisted and cold, Tanya chewing hangnails as they had interrogated her, Ben hovering over Milo at the bottom of the steps yesterday. How to put all this together? "Sometimes I get the feeling that there's a whole lot more going on with this than just our finding a murderer."

"I think you might be right. But that is not a comforting thought." Keir lifted both shoulders, and then went on, "There still is a lot of activity out at the Leahy house. I've been so busy with the break-ins, robberies and trying to solve Ginger's murder that I really haven't had time to set up a drug bust."

"I need you to go with me to talk to Sylvie," Ridge began. There was a knock at the door. He turned and saw Sylvie, standing on the other side of the window in the door. Lovely as usual, she entered. But he could tell she was masking her own tension. A smile hovered around her lips, but on this sunny morning her eyes were a moody dark violet. She was the last person he wanted to see here today. He grimaced, but stood and opened the door for her.

"Good morning." Sylvie greeted the two of them but she sent Ridge a wry grin. "I'm glad to find you two together." She sat down in the chair that the sheriff offered her. "Has Ridge told you what I think I should do?"

The sheriff lifted one eyebrow. "No, we haven't had the chance to talk about you as yet."

Ridge sat down in the chair closest to the door, beside Sylvie's. While he felt grim, she was sounding lighthearted. He wished he had something in hand to crush. How could he get through to her about how dangerous her plan was? "She wants," Ridge said bluntly, "to move into Ginger's apartment and be bait to trap the murderer."

The sheriff raised his eyebrows even higher this time. "Where did that come from?"

"Last night," Sylvie said as she sat back, getting more comfortable in her chair, "I finally realized that I might be putting my father and Ben in danger by staying in my own apartment."

"I thought she'd finally seen some sense." Ridge let his disgust over this ridiculous idea resonate in every word. "But then she came up with this idea that she should be bait."

The sheriff did not react right away. He steepled his fingers and gazed at the two of them.

Ridge did not appreciate his hesitation. Sylvie's sweet fragrance floated to him as if trying to soften him, make him lose his focus.

"I can understand," the sheriff spoke slowly, "why Ridge would be unhappy about this suggestion of yours, Sylvie. But we might have to resort to this if we can get no further in this case."

Ridge was on his feet before he realized he was moving. "Over my dead body." Anger blazed white-hot through him.

The sheriff held up one hand, motioned Ridge to sit down. "I only said, *might*. You and I both know that Sylvie is in danger already as matters stand. We could lay a trap—"

"No!" Ridge thundered.

Sylvie did not move, did not look at Ridge. "I realize that you just want to protect me, Ridge. But I am a grown woman. And Ginger was my cousin." Then Sylvie's voice dropped in pitch and lifted in urgency. "We have to find out who killed her. He can't walk scot-free. I want justice. Not revenge. Justice."

Ridge fisted his hands to keep from grabbing her shoulders to shake some sense into her.

"Sylvie," the sheriff said, fingering some papers on his desk, "let me think about this. Don't do anything until we've discussed it and decided on a plan."

"Thank you, Sheriff, for taking me seriously." She glanced at Ridge, her eyes pleading with him. "I'm not doing this just to flout you, Ridge. We must bring this dreadful mystery to an end. There must come a time—soon—when it is over, settled. I don't want this to be one of those cases where twenty years later the truth is uncovered. I want the truth now."

Ridge had spent most of the rest of the day working with the sheriff on getting evidence against Keski, hoping against hope that this would somehow tie in with Ginger's case. Sylvie's plan had plagued him all day and he had been trying to come up with a way to prevent her from doing anything so ill-advised as offering herself as bait.

In the end, the prosecuting attorney had decided that, with Keski's long criminal record, they had enough to get a court order for a DNA sample and a search warrant for Keski's dilapidated trailer. Especially since the barkeep at Bugsy's had testified in a signed statement that after the robbery, the robber must have driven off in Keski's truck.

With preparing the case in mind, the sheriff had had Keski tailed from the time he'd finished questioning him and let him go home the night before. Keski had not left the trailer since then. And no one had been to visit him.

The long process finished and in the waning daylight, Ridge got into his SUV to go to Shirley's house, feeling years older than he had just this morning. Shirley had invited him along with Sylvie and Ben for supper to welcome Milo home from the hospital. As he headed to pick up Sylvie at her bookshop first, his cell phone rang. He flipped it open. "Matthews here."

"Block here. We've just had a triple murder in Madison. I need you back here. It's been around what? Three weeks since that Winfield murder? I don't think that case is going to break. How soon can you be back in Madison?" Ridge's boss went on before he could respond, "I need you ASAP."

The rapid-fire delivery left Ridge speechless for a moment or two. "ASAP?"

"Yes, I could use you tomorrow morning. This is a high-profile murder. A state congressman is implicated."

There was really only one answer Ridge could give Block. He gave it. As he drove toward Sylvie's bookstore, he clenched his hands around the steering wheel. His quota of worry suddenly maxed out. He was leaving and Sylvie had an idiotic idea that could conceivably get her killed. The sheriff hadn't backed him up, either. How could he persuade Sylvie not to go ahead with her baiting-a-trap idea?

Then a notion that had been simmering in the back of his mind moved to the forefront. When he'd first thought of it, he'd dismissed it immediately. But the notion had become more insistent and more persistent. He didn't know if she would go for it. The thought of putting this into words made him uncomfortable. But he would do anything to protect Sylvie. If nothing else, it might distract her from her plan. It really made good sense in several ways. He steeled himself to suggest it. *Nothing ventured; nothing gained.*

Walking into Sylvie's store, he was relieved to find her alone. He didn't want to ask her this unless they were guaranteed to be alone, completely alone. "Is your dad home safe, then?" As had become usual, being near Sylvie heightened his awareness. Each time he saw her, it was as if he were seeing her for the first time. And each time he found something about her he had never noticed. This time he noticed that she had one golden freckle probably left over from summer at the outer side of her right eye. In his mind, he pressed his lips to that soft spot.

"Dad's at Shirley's already." She looked into his eyes as if trying to read his mind. How was it that she always seemed to sense things about him?

It made him edgy. "Good." He stopped speaking, gathering up his nerve. He fought the urge to draw her to her feet and into his arms. Maybe this all stemmed from what he planned to ask her.

"What is it, Ridge?" she asked without preamble.

Before he could lose his nerve, he said in a rush, "Sylvie, we've always been good friends. Haven't we?" He hurried on, not giving her a chance to speak. "These past few weeks have opened my eyes. I was wondering if you would consider marrying me."

* * *

Sylvie couldn't breathe. Not even in her wildest daydreams had she guessed that Ridge's feelings toward her had changed. And as she gazed at him now, she did not see standing before her a man in love. For several moments, she made herself remain still. It was hard to keep her tongue behind her teeth. She'd realized then to what painful extent her feelings for Ridge had come alive again over the past month. *I am in love with him,* she now admitted silently.

This wasn't cause for jubilation. In spite of Ridge's few recent expressions of attraction to her—their few kisses—she didn't believe that he had deep feelings for her. Or it might be that he did not realize that he had deep feelings for her. But that point was moot.

"Tell me what you mean, Ridge."

"I want you to marry me." He sounded put-upon, not ardent.

"No, you don't want to marry me," she said calmly, slowly shredding the tissue she'd pulled from a box on her desk. "Is this a way to persuade me not to move into Ginger's apartment?"

Ridge's face twisted with dismay.

Unhappy to be proved correct, she went on, "Ridge, I know you. You're not a man in love. Why not try to be honest with me?"

"This isn't difficult," he persisted. "I think we should get married."

She wouldn't take this seriously, wouldn't let it upset her. *He's just trying to protect me.* "Why should we get married?"

He made a sound of irritation. "This isn't twenty questions."

"It may become that if you don't tell me plainly what you're talking about." She folded her arms and stared at him. As always, his presence was formidable. He wasn't a man to give up on anything easily.

He paced back and forth in front of her a few times. Then he stopped and turned toward her. "I know that we have not really been dating or anything. But I have gotten the feeling a few times over the last couple of weeks that you were attracted to me and I have had that same feeling…same attraction for you…at the same times."

If she didn't take into consideration how well-intentioned his clumsy proposal was, she could have chuckled at this lame attempt. She remained silent, merely sitting back and gazing up at him.

He did not look at her. "I need someone to help me with Ben. I'm tired of living alone. I like you and respect you. Will you marry me?"

She'd longed to hear these words from him. Never thought she would hear them from anyone. But in this situation, they fell sadly flat. He sounded as if he were giving the reasons for making a purchase, not proposing marriage. "No, Ridge, I won't marry you."

"But it makes such good sense."

"To you, perhaps." This time a smile did curve her mouth. *Men.* "But I get the feeling that you have an agenda that you're not telling me about. I already suggested that you're doing this in some way to talk me out of helping the sheriff catch Ginger's murderer."

"That's right. I don't want you to be used as bait. But how could a marriage proposal from me make you change that?"

She decided to use his own question, his own words to make her argument for her. "Thank you for stating my point so succinctly. What do you want?"

He made a sound of frustration and began pacing again. "I've been thinking about your hip. If you married me, you would be covered by my group insurance. You'd be able to get your hip replacement. And I already told you that I need help with Ben. You would make him a very good mother and Milo would be his grandfather then. It all makes perfect sense, doesn't it?"

Sylvie sighed. She could get very affronted if she let herself. But what was the point? It was obvious that he was not being honest with her or with himself. But she couldn't change that.

She glanced at the wall clock. "We are expected at Shirley's now. Let's get going." She stood and started toward the hall tree to get her coat.

"You haven't given me your answer," he insisted.

"Ridge, when you can tell me honestly that you

love me and that I am the only woman you will ever love then I might say yes. Until then, I plan to forget that we had this conversation."

Ridge exclaimed in an undertone something that sounded like, "Women."

Sylvie felt a sudden rush of emotion that she had tried to hold back. She blinked it away and went about pulling on her plum-colored tam and letting Ridge help her with her coat. His hands brushed her shoulders and she nearly caved in and burrowed into his embrace. *But, no.* He was still clueless. And would probably remain that way. *I won't let this hurt my feelings. I will not.*

To help her get herself back under control, she said to Ridge, "I keep thinking about Tanya Hendricks. How is she doing after being held up?"

# TEN

Ridge couldn't decide whether Sylvie had brought up the discussion of Tanya just to distract him or if she thought the girl was important to Ginger's case. Had he missed something? To him, the girl was troubling, but so far he'd not found any way to connect her to Ginger except for the fact that Tanya had spoken to Ginger on the night she died.

Ridge wasn't any closer to knowing how to protect Sylvie. She obviously hadn't bought his proposal. What was so odd about his proposing? She hadn't even taken him seriously. That stung.

Disgruntled, he walked beside Sylvie up the walk. Snow had melted and was now refreezing. Shirley and Tom's back door loomed above—shining with a welcoming light. In one way, he looked forward to a relaxed evening with such good people.

But in another, he was tired, so very tired of all this uncertainty and unexpected emotion. Even his parents' silent home appealed to him now. There he could just sit, wordless and unnoticed. But he might not go there tonight at all. A new idea had just come to him. Someone, and evidently it would be him, had to do something.

Ridge followed Sylvie through Tom and Shirley's back door. And realized that he should not have come. Realized it immediately.

"—Rae-Jean," Chaney was pleading, "I'm not asking for anything you couldn't do—"

"How many times do I have to tell you?" Rae-Jean asked, sounding desperate, stormy. "I'm too weak yet. I don't trust myself."

Rae-Jean and Chaney sat at Shirley's kitchen table. When Rae-Jean glimpsed Sylvie behind Chaney, she stood up, pushing her chair back.

Chaney grabbed Rae-Jean's hand. "Please—"

"We're not alone." Rae-Jean pulled her hand from his grasp.

Ridge had hung back behind Sylvie. But now over Sylvie's shoulder, he saw Tom and Shirley appear in the opposite doorway. Ridge took a step back. This wasn't his family. He shouldn't be here.

Sylvie took a step forward. "Rae-Jean, don't send Chaney away. Ridge and I will leave."

Ridge put a hand on Sylvie's shoulder, trying to restrain her. *Stay back. This doesn't involve us, you.*

Chaney turned sideways and addressed everyone. "Please don't leave. I've been trying to persuade Rae-Jean to go to counseling with me.

And our business isn't really private. Everyone in town is talking about it."

"Do you have to remind me?" Rae-Jean demanded, pushing her abundant blond hair off her face with one hand. "Jake's teacher already called me to tell me that she thinks he needs counseling. Because of all the stuff kids have repeated to him about me. Stuff that they've overheard from their parents. Maybe I shouldn't have come back to Winfield. But I didn't have anywhere else to go." She turned away, hunching over as if hiding tears.

Shirley hurried to Rae-Jean's side and put an arm around her. "The important thing is you are here. That you are getting better every day."

"I don't see myself getting better every day," Rae-Jean said like a fretful child, laying her forehead against Shirley's shoulder.

"I'm glad that Chaney has finally suggested that the two of you seek counseling," Sylvie said, moving toward Rae-Jean, slipping from Ridge's loose grip. "Why aren't you willing to let things get better? Why are you holding on to your guilt?"

Ridge marveled at the love they were showing this sad woman who had made such a mess of her life.

"I am guilty," Rae-Jean snapped. "I can't forget what I've done."

"Rae-Jean, listen to me," Sylvie said, moving forward another step. "I felt terrible guilt for a very long time after Dan died that night—"

"But that was an accident!" Rae-Jean objected.

Sylvie reached out for Rae-Jean's hand and caught it. "We were fighting. Dan was trying to tell me what to do. And I wasn't going to let a boy tell me what to do. He pushed me and I pushed him and the railing behind us broke…." On the last word, her voice cracked.

Ridge saw the starch go out of Sylvie. He moved forward and put his arm around her. Hearing her account of his brother's death had grabbed his heart. He'd never realized that Sylvie had struggled with guilt over Dan's death. Just as he did. Still.

"Rae-Jean, I understand guilt." Sylvie spoke in a soft and understanding voice. "It can destroy your life. Don't let it do that to you. Turn it over to God like I did. Let Him free you."

Ridge's stomach churned. If it were only that easy.

For a few moments, no one moved. No one spoke. Then Rae-Jean said, "None of you know what drugs can do to a person. Make a person do." She pulled away from Shirley and headed toward the front hall.

"I'm not giving up on you, Rae-Jean," Chaney called after her. "Not while we still have our children to think of. You screwed up one year of your life and that shouldn't ruin the rest of it for both of us."

"None of you know what I've done!" Rae-Jean called over her shoulder as she left the room.

In the past few moments, Ridge's respect for

Chaney Franklin had expanded exponentially.
And Sylvie's words and Rae-Jean's echoed in
Ridge's mind. *Let Him free you. None of you
know what I've done!*

She sat huddled on the cluttered floor of her
room. She hadn't thought things could get any
worse. But somehow they had. Why couldn't they
understand what she was going through? Everyone
thought she should just be happy and go on with
life. They kept saying, you're young, you have your
whole life ahead of you. *Yeah, right.*

And then the bedroom carpet under her began to
buck. The desk lamp burst into green and purple
flame. She squeezed her eyes shut, but that didn't
shut out the sensations. They weren't coming from
outside her, but from inside. She clamped her hands
over her mouth to keep from screaming. How much
longer could she survive this?

Later that night at home when the darkened
apartment was quiet, Sylvie got up. She'd waited
until she was sure that her father and Ben were
sound asleep. She couldn't fall asleep. Not with
Ridge leaving in the morning. Not after he had
proposed to her. Not after she had witnessed the
conflict between Chaney and Rae-Jean.

Sylvie walked silently to the large windows overlooking the harbor. Midnight radiance attracted her,

the half-moon and stars above. Lights from Madeleine Island glowed across the harbor. The street below and northern horizon were illumined as all these light sources were reflected by the snow and ice, a natural halo effect.

She pulled her robe tighter at the neck against the nighttime chill radiating from the large windows. What was she going to do about Ridge's proposal? Because if she knew one thing about Ridge, he wouldn't take her rebuff for a final answer. He would pursue her unless she thought of a way to stop him.

Never in a million years would she have expected Ridge to propose to her. And in fact, he hadn't really proposed to her. He had offered her what, in the past, had been called a marriage of convenience. She'd been right to refuse. But perhaps she shouldn't dismiss it completely from her mind. Couldn't dismiss him.

Tonight his presence behind her, backing her up, had given her the courage to tell Rae-Jean the truth about her feelings of guilt over Dan. Tonight when he'd brought her home, what would he have done if she'd leaned over and kissed him? Just kissed him good-night? She closed her eyes, imagining his arms closing around her and him returning her kiss.

She bent her head forward to press it against the cold window glass. When she had been a little girl and had a fever, she'd often done this to make herself feel better. It didn't work anymore. Her chaotic thoughts pounded against her skull as if trying to break through. Did Ridge's proposal signify anything? Perhaps he was changing.

He certainly wouldn't have proposed even a marriage of convenience to her nearly three weeks ago. Perhaps Ginger's murder, the break-ins, Rae-Jean and Chaney's dilemma and finally the recent attack on her father and Ben had succeeded in chipping through his outer veneer. Outside the window on the dark expanse that was the frozen rim of Lake Superior, she tracked the headlights of a few vehicles heading east.

When would the ice break? When would the secret of Ginger's death be cracked to reveal the facts? When would God's truth penetrate Ridge's sorrow and self-reproach? And was there anything she could do to help him break free of the past?

A thought occurred to her, but did she have the nerve to carry it out?

From his SUV parked farther down the waterfront street, Ridge glimpsed Sylvie pressing her face against the front window of her apartment. Couldn't she sleep? Would she see him down here? He shifted on his seat. Then his saw a deputy's Jeep approaching from the opposite direction. The deputy parked and flashed his headlights. Once. Ridge started his car. And flashed his headlights once in return.

Ridge had persuaded Keir to station someone

outside Sylvie's apartment at night. Ridge had done the first shift. Now at midnight he could drive home, leaving Sylvie with another law officer's surveillance. He needed sleep. Tomorrow, he had to drive to Madison. Never had that thought left him feeling so bleak.

*March 22*

Just after dawn the next morning, a groggy Ridge stood looking around his room at his parents' house. Had he left anything? Just then, his mother appeared in the doorway. "I found these on top of the dryer in the laundry room. I must have forgotten to put them with your other things." She handed him a stack of neatly folded underwear and T-shirts.

"Thanks, Mom." He took the stack of clothing from her hand and set it in his open suitcase, distributing it to make an even pile.

His mother did not immediately leave as he would have expected her to. As she always did.

"It's been nice having you home," she said.

He paused in the midst of his chore and turned to look at her. Neither of his parents had said words like this to him in nearly twenty years. He couldn't say that it had been nice being here. Because it had been uncomfortable and unpleasant to live with his silent, self-contained parents over the past weeks.

It had been years since he had spent more than a

day or two at home with his parents. Maybe he was to blame for part of their disconnection. But now he must say something. What? After a moment's thought, he said, "Thanks, Mom."

She nodded and turned away, walking back to the living room where the early-morning show had kicked off her day of TV.

After a solitary breakfast, Ridge packed up his car and drove to Milo's apartment to say goodbye to Ben, Milo and Sylvie. As he walked up the steps to their door, he thought of the attack on Milo. So much had transpired in three short weeks. *I will call Keir before I leave town to check once more that Sylvie still has round-the-clock protection.* But he couldn't leave without saying goodbye.

He knocked on the door and Sylvie opened it. She was already dressed for her day at work. She wore a vivid lavender corduroy jacket and matching slacks and looked beautiful as usual. Out of the blue, his mind brought up the image of him taking Sylvie with him to Madison and introducing her to his colleagues as his fiancée.

Imagining their surprised expressions, he knew he would be the object of general envy. What was wrong with Winfield? Every man over thirty here had to be blind not to notice how beautiful Sylvie was. All this clotted together in his throat and made it difficult for him to speak. But he managed to say, "Good morning, Sylvie."

"Good morning," she replied and waved him inside. "Have you eaten?"

"Yes, I just came to tell Ben that I would be back as soon as I can and to obey you and Milo while I'm gone."

"I'm sure Ben will be no problem to us," Milo replied, sitting at the table with his Bible open.

"I'll be good," Ben said, swallowing the last spoonful of his Corn Flakes.

"Ridge, why don't you sit down with us for a moment?" Milo invited. "Ben was just going to read our Bible verse for today."

Ridge found that, while reading the Bible before beginning the day was not his usual custom, he wanted to linger here for just a few moments longer. "Okay." He sat down in the chair next to Ben and accepted a cup of coffee from Sylvie.

Ben picked up the large black book and read:

"Matthew 6:18-20, Do not store up for yourselves treasures on earth, where moth and rust destroy, and where thieves break in and steal. But store up for yourselves treasures in heaven, where moth and rust do not destroy, and where thieves do not break in and steal."

"Now, Ben, read 1 Timothy 6:10-11," Milo instructed, indicating a bookmark. After using the mark to find his place, Ben obeyed, reading:

"For the love of money is a root of all kinds of evil. Some people, eager for money, have wandered from the faith and pierced themselves with many griefs."

"What do you think that means, Ben?" Milo asked.

"We're not supposed to be greedy?" Ben replied.

"Excellent answer," Milo said, patting the boy's arm. "You'll hear people say that money is the root of all evil. But remember that Paul told Timothy that it was the root of all kinds of evil. There are many sources of evil or perhaps many ways to fall into evil."

"Do you think someone killed Ginger because of money?" the boy asked.

"We don't know yet," Milo said, "why Ginger was taken from us. I hope that we will someday."

Ridge hoped it wasn't his own guilty conscience projecting his feelings onto Milo. But had Milo given up on Ridge discovering who Ginger's murderer was? The thought iced his inner core. Ridge sipped the last of Sylvie's good coffee in his cup and rose. "I need to get going. I won't reach Madison until late afternoon as it is."

Sylvie rose and offered him her soft, slender hand. "Drive safely."

Milo and Ben also rose and shook hands with Ridge. "Don't worry about us," Milo assured him. "We'll be fine."

"Yeah," Ben echoed, "we'll be fine."

Ridge wished that he could be as confident of that as they were.

"I'll walk you down to your vehicle," Milo said. "Ben, you go gather up your books and I'll drive you to school today."

Ridge had the unusual urge to turn back and kiss Sylvie goodbye. This more than anything told him it was time, way past time, for him to get out of Winfield. And he didn't think Milo escorting him down to his car was just politeness. What did Milo want? Surely Sylvie hadn't told Milo about Ridge's proposal to her?

As he walked down to his SUV, Ridge was aware that the wind had softened. The warm front that the weatherman had been promising must have moved in. There was even the scent of rain in the air. But Ridge had grown up in Winfield and he knew how fickle the weather could be. The scent of rain could pass and a blizzard could follow.

Milo didn't keep Ridge guessing about the reason why he had walked down with him. When Ridge reached his vehicle, Milo said, "Ridge, what do you think about letting me adopt Ben?"

Ridge was completely caught off guard. He'd thought Milo would have something to say about the case Ridge had been investigating for most of March. "Adopt Ben?" he repeated. "How did you come up with that?"

"Ben and I have really hit it off. I know that I am

some twenty years older than you, but I think Ben and I would get along fine. And you've said yourself that your lifestyle is not conducive to parenting. But mine is. I have a lot of time for Ben. He would be with me in the store during the summers and school holidays." Milo leaned against Ridge's SUV.

Ridge couldn't think of a word to say.

Milo continued, "Ben suffered great injury, losing his parents at such a tender age, and he needs someone who can devote time to him. I have the time. And I like Ben. I could easily come to love him. I've been kind of holding back from letting him know that, since I thought you would be taking him from us. But I want him. Will you consider it?"

Ridge instantly became aware of his ambivalence about Ben. He hadn't wanted the responsibility of Ben. He'd tried to shift the care of Ben to boarding school and summer camp. But now that Milo was offering to take Ben and raise him as his own, Ridge felt a sense of loss. He pushed it aside. "I will think about it, Milo." They shook hands and Ridge got into his vehicle and slammed the door.

As he drove out of town, he felt some emotion inside him growing, increasing, inflating. What was this awful feeling? No answer came to him. He flipped open his cell phone and speed-dialed the sheriff's number. "Matthews here. I'm on my way out of town. Has anything happened since we last talked?"

"No, unfortunately nothing," Keir answered.

"Will you promise me to keep a close watch on Sylvie while I'm gone?" Ridge requested. There was a pause that Ridge did not like. "Keir?" he prompted.

"I know you won't like this, Ridge," Keir said, "but I am seriously considering Sylvie's offer to move into Ginger's apartment as bait."

"You can't be serious. We're dealing with a murderer." Ridge felt his pulse accelerating. He wanted to yell into the phone, curse the sheriff. "You wouldn't let your wife, Audra, take such a risk, would you?" he demanded hotly.

There was another pause on the line. Then the sheriff said in an odd tone, "That is a very interesting question, a very interesting comparison."

Then Ridge could hear muffled sounds as if the sheriff must be talking to someone with his face away from the phone.

"Call me when you have a chance, Ridge," Keir said, coming back on the line. "I have to get busy now."

"Has something popped up?"

"No, nothing you need to be worried about. Good luck with your triple murder in Madison. Give my thanks to Block when you see him." Keir hung up.

Ridge snapped his phone shut in anger. Why had the sheriff thought his question *interesting?* Ridge turned onto the highway and faced south. Then the sensation came again like pulling against bindings or a tow rope. It was as if Winfield were trying to tow him back. But he had no choice. He had to return to his job, his life.

He sipped the last of the cheap whiskey. Nothing had gone right in his life for a very long time now. And none of it was his fault. Just one unlucky break after another. If he didn't have bad luck, he would have no luck at all. And that wasn't funny. If he didn't turn things around within the next few days, it would all be over for good. They'd probably find his body floating in Lake Superior. This thought filled him with stark, icy terror. He clutched the slippery shot glass. He felt that he might be sick to his stomach. *How can I turn this around? I've done everything I could. And it has been one disaster after another.*

There was only one answer. He'd have to grab the girl. There was no other way.

As soon as he accepted this line of thought, he began to plan his strategy. Maybe he could get what he wanted from her without killing her. He hadn't planned on killing the first time. The thought of killing someone in cold blood filled him with the same kind of terror as the image of his own body floating facedown.

But he couldn't waste any more time. And if it were a choice between someone else's life and his, he would have no trouble choosing his own life first.

\* \* \*

In Madison late that afternoon, Ridge sat around a table with several other homicide detectives. Block stood at the end of the table beside a dry erase board and was going over the different measures their department had already taken toward solving the triple murder.

All around him, his fellow officers were jotting down notes, compiling information. Ridge knew that at the end of this informational presentation they would be asked to come up with some new ideas for pursuing more information to solve these murders. But Ridge's mind was still in Winfield.

Sylvie's face, and then Milo asking to let him adopt Ben, and finally his last conversation with the sheriff. Why had Keir thought Ridge's comparing Audra and Sylvie odd?

"Matthews, you have anything to contribute?" Block asked him.

Jerked back to the present, he was caught unprepared. "Not right now."

Block eyed him. "You don't see anything that we might have missed? I was hoping you would bring a new perspective."

Ridge shook his head, not liking the fact that everyone was gazing at him. His neck warmed just under his collar.

"Well," Block said, "let it percolate overnight. And tomorrow, you will visit the crime scene. And we should have all the results from the forensic tests by then. We'll have more to work with."

Ridge, along with everyone else, pushed back his chairs and surged to his feet. It was nearly time for the day to end. Ridge returned to his office and looked at his oddly unfamiliar desk. He should feel right at home here. But he felt strange, as if he had become an alien to these surroundings. He'd only been away nearly three weeks. He sat down and tried to think what to do. He began going through the neat paper-clipped files on top of his desk, trying to reorient himself.

He recognized his handwriting on his papers but he still felt as if he were a stranger sitting at someone else's desk. *It will just take me a few days to get back into the flow. That's all.* But Sylvie's face popped into his mind again, her wispy fringe of bangs, her fair skin. He imagined stroking her soft cheek and trailing his fingers through her short hair. He closed his eyes, banishing her from his mind. And then he opened his eyes and resumed going through his files. *Snap out of it, Ridge. Get a grip.*

Later that night, the phone rang at Keir and Audra's house. "Sheriff, this is Ollie."

From Ollie's tone, Keir did not expect this to be a social call. He could hear Audra saying good-night to their little girl, Evie, in her bedroom. "What can I do for you, Ollie?"

"My granddaughter is missing. I think she might have run away."

*Great.* "Did she leave a note?"

"No," the older man said, sounding distracted, "I tried to look for one in her stuff. And, Sheriff, I think you need to come and look at Tanya's room."

"What's in her room?"

"Just come. It makes me sick."

# ELEVEN

Ridge sat in his silent apartment. In front of him on the dusty coffee table, he riffled a stack of bills to pay. And he had so many other chores to do. He'd spent the whole day investigating the triple-murder crime scene and trying to keep his mind nailed to it. But it had been a futile exercise.

His mind had kept returning to his North Star, which had become Sylvie, Ben and everyone up in Winfield. He closed his eyes and pinched the bridge of his nose, trying to relieve the unrelenting pressure he felt.

Still, he'd put off calling Sylvie as long as he could stand it. Because yesterday, he had realized how much he had not wanted to leave her. Surrendering, he dialed her number. It rang six times and then she picked up, sounding breathless. "Hello, this is Sylvie."

"It's Ridge." Then he couldn't think of what he wanted to say to her. Or was it that he knew what he wanted to say to her but he couldn't say it? He pinched the bridge of his nose again.

"Oh, hi," she said.

Her tone was not welcoming. Was she upset that he'd left her immediately after proposing marriage? But she hadn't taken his proposal seriously at all. That still stung. "How are you?"

"Fine."

Why was she acting as though he were a stranger? The memory of her soft lips made his own tingle. "How are things?" he asked, realizing how inadequate his own words were.

"The ice is beginning to crack near Washburn."

*I didn't call for a weather report. I could look that up on the Internet.* "I mean," he said with emphasis, "how are things with the case?"

"Didn't the sheriff call you?" She sounded miffed with him. Why?

Ridge began to steam. "No, he didn't call me. Why should he have called me?"

"Well, maybe he didn't think that it…it had anything to do with Ginger's case. But I think it might."

*All right. Just tell me.* "What's happened?" he asked, holding on to his irritation with both hands and clenched teeth.

"Tanya Hendricks, you remember who—"

Why was she acting as if he'd lost all memory of Winfield in a mere twenty-four hours? "Yes," he said emphatically, "I know who Tanya Hendricks is. Now what's happened to her?"

"They think she's run away."

"She's missing?" He sat up straighter.

"That's right. And, well, I know you hate gossip. But rumor has it that all kinds of drugs—LSD, marijuana and amphetamines, I think—were found in her room at Ollie's house. I guess Ollie is pretty shook up."

This was not news to him. He'd read the signs of drug abuse when he'd watched Keir question the girl. Ridge rubbed his taut forehead. "Does the sheriff have any leads about where she might have gone?"

"They've talked to her stepfather, that Jim Leahy that you and the sheriff went to serve a search warrant on. But he says he hasn't seen the girl for months. Not since her mother dumped him and then dumped Tanya on her grandfather, Ollie. Keir and Ollie have tried to contact Tanya's mother. But she's somewhere in the south of France and they couldn't get hold of her."

Sylvie's concern for this young girl, whom she hardly knew, glistened in every word. His voice softened. "Do they think the Hendricks girl was snatched? Or did she just run away?"

"They really don't know. They've put out an APB because she took nothing with her. I would have thought that you might have heard about that." Sylvie sounded distracted. Had Tanya's disappearance increased her own unspoken fear?

"No, I've been buried with this case." He was stuck here and she needed him. "It's really messy." That was putting it mildly. He was glad that when they found Ginger, there hadn't been any blood.

"Do you want to talk to Ben?"

*No, I want to talk to you. Really talk. To you. Just you.* Did being in Madison separate him so completely from her? Or was she upset because he had returned to his home in Madison? Everything had become tangled in a confused mess. A headache was beginning at the back of his neck.

"Ridge?" she prompted.

"Is Ben near the phone?" Ridge tried not to sound aggravated, though he was.

"Come here, Ben," she summoned. "Ridge is on the phone and wants to say hi." Then she was off the line. Beyond his reach. That cost him an unexpected sharp pang. He massaged the center of his chest with the heel of one hand, trying to soothe the tension building there. He made small talk with Ben for a while and then he asked for Sylvie again.

"She's gone downstairs," Ben reported. "Here's Milo."

This felt like she was definitely avoiding him. Ridge tasted sour acid on his tongue. Was Sylvie avoiding him? But he did not ask that of Milo. They made small talk for a few moments.

Then Ridge said, "I'm going to try to get off on the weekend to come up for a visit."

"Watch the weather reports," Milo cautioned him. "There's a lot of activity overhead—coming and going. And you know how unsettled March can be."

It was as if everybody in the Patterson household was warning him away. When had he become persona non grata? "I'll keep that in mind, Milo. Take care." He hung up before he said anything more about Sylvie.

Altogether a completely unsatisfactory phone conversation. He massaged the back of his neck, and then stretched his aching head in every direction. The words he had exchanged with Sylvie put him in mind of his weekly conversations with his parents—where they completely disconnected from him, leaving him "outside."

Without hesitation, he dialed Keir's home number. And then without preamble, he asked, "What's this I hear about Tanya Hendricks running away?"

"Oh," the sheriff replied, "I didn't expect to hear from you so soon."

*Obviously.* "What's this I hear about the Hendricks girl running away?" Ridge repeated, tapping the coffee table with his fingertips, making divots in the dust.

"Ollie called me last night. The girl didn't show up to relieve the day person at the convenience store." The sheriff sounded as if he was reporting the case to someone he didn't know. Ridge's fingertips tapped faster and harder. "Tanya hasn't made many friends here, but Ollie called a few people who knew her. Without any luck—"

"I heard they found drugs in her room," Ridge interrupted.

"Evidently Winfield gossip has traveled all the way down to Madison, too," Keir observed wryly.

"Sylvie told me." Her name caught in his throat. "Who do you think Tanya's supplier is? Maybe her stepfather?"

"Well, there are several possibilities. As soon as I find the girl—that's our main priority right now, of course. After I find her, then I'm going to set up a drug bust at Leahy's. I've put it off too long because of Ginger's murder investigation. I can't get rid of drugs completely. But I need to keep the pressure on the local dealers. I can't let them get cocky."

"I hear you." Ridge racked his brain for some suggestion to offer the sheriff about finding Tanya. But he came up with nada. He stopped tapping the table and flexed his fist. He changed subjects. "Have you been able to arrest Doyle Keski yet?"

"You've only been gone one day," the sheriff chided. "I just took the DNA sample from him yesterday. It will take a while for the lab to identify it as a match or not with the cells left in the snowmobiling mask."

Ridge swallowed his irritation. "What I had in mind was—when you used the search warrant we got, did you find the money from Bugsy's in Keski's trailer?"

"No luck there. And believe me, we searched. And his trailer was like a condemned landfill." Keir revealed his disgust with his voice. "It took hours to search."

Keir cleared his throat. "I know you won't like this. But I want to warn you. I am getting serious about setting Sylvie up as bait—"

"You are right." Ridge wished he could reach through the phone and shake some sense into the man. "I don't want to hear that. I think doing that is completely irresponsible. It's taking an unacceptable risk."

"And I think you're deluding yourself. As a law enforcement professional, you know that it is the easiest way to flush out our culprit. But you're in love with Sylvie Patterson and you refuse to admit it."

Keir's unforeseen words drenched Ridge like ice-cold water in his face. He almost sputtered out the first words—ones of staunch denial. But just in time, he caught himself before he said anything he would regret. "Well, keep me posted. And before you set up your trap with Sylvie as bait, I'll expect you to give me advance warning."

"Will do."

Was he imagining it or did Keir sound amused? "Fine," Ridge snapped and hung up.

*March 24*

The sheriff drove slowly down the highway that followed the line of the shore of Lake Superior. Tanya Hendricks had been missing now for two days. Even though he should be on his way home he couldn't shake the idea that the key to finding the girl had something to do with her stepfather.

He did not like Jim Leahy. It was a gut reaction and when it came to assessing people, he had learned to trust his gut. There was something furtive and underhanded about Leahy. The man might even be responsible for Tanya's disappearance. And he may have left some clue of her whereabouts near his home. Keir slowed to let a deer pass in front of him.

Wisps of mist floated up from the shore. Warm air had blown in and it was moving across the frozen surface of the lake, forming fog. The snow had melted over the last week, shrinking mounds and revealing brown, strawlike grass. And as Keir drove slowly down the highway behind the Leahy place, he glimpsed a private lane, which the snow had hidden before. It looked as if it followed the western perimeter of the Leahy property.

Keir slowed and turned in. He would drive as far as the snow would permit him and then he would give up for the night and go home. His deputy Josh would be searching for the girl on every dead-end road and in every hunting shack in the county tonight. He entered the lane and drove slowly.

Ahead, near a clump of trees, he glimpsed a strange mound on the ground. Rags? Keir blinked his eyes. No one would leave a bundle of rags out here in the snow mounds. Maybe it was just a pile of soggy autumn leaves. The bundle or pile or whatever it was moved. An animal? Or the lost girl?

He slowed and halted. Getting out, he started for the pile. It growled. A small, dirty white dog appeared from the pile and barked at him. Keir shook his head and turned to go.

The small dog pursued him—yapping. Keir ignored him, but the dog didn't give up. Finally the little pest sank his teeth into Keir's pant leg. "What!" Keir tried to shake the dog off. The little ball of fur wouldn't let go. "Get! Get off me!"

The dog began to tug at Keir, as if trying to pull him back toward the heap. Keir stopped. This dog wasn't trying to be irritating; he wanted Keir to go to the heap of leaves. And wasn't this the dog he'd seen at Leahy's? Keir turned back and gazed at the leaves. They moved again. "Okay, fella, what's this all about?"

The dog yapped excitedly and bounded back toward the pile of leaves. Keir began walking and then running. He dropped to his knees in the melting snow beside the pine trees. Under the leaves lay Tanya Hendricks.

For one second, he feared that she was dead. Then he remembered he had seen movement. He found her pulse, but it was weak and so very slow. He gathered her into his arms. He looked around for the dog but it had disappeared. He didn't have time for another mystery. But when he had time, he would find out who definitely owned the little white dog who had pointed the way to the girl. And saved her life, Keir hoped as he punched dispatch's number into his cell phone.

*March 25*

Sylvie couldn't believe what the sheriff had told her. Why would Tanya Hendricks want to speak to her? But here she was Friday morning at eleven o'clock walking beside him down the polished linoleum hallway on the second floor of the Ashford Hospital. They paused at the end of the corridor at a glass partition and doorway.

The nurse at the glass partition smiled at the sheriff, rose and opened the secured door for them.

The sheriff nodded his thanks. "This is Sylvie Patterson. She's with me."

"You're in luck," the nurse said. "Tanya's been with the psychiatrist. He has been assessing her. But I think he's finished with her."

"I have a court order to talk with him, too."

The nurse agreed to arrange it. And after a quick phone call, she gave him directions to the psychiatrist's office downstairs. But first she led him and Sylvie to Tanya's bedside. Tanya was in a semiprivate room, but the other patient was out.

"Hello, Tanya," Sylvie said when the nurse left them. The sheriff hung back by the doorway.

The young girl in a drab hospital gown looked at Sylvie. "I know who you are," Tanya said in a very frail voice. The girl was skeletally thin.

"Yes, I run the bookstore." Sylvie sat down on the edge of the bedside chair.

The girl's hair was clean but flattened as if someone had washed it and merely combed it back. She gazed at Sylvie, her eyes underscored by gray shadows.

Sylvie offered what she hoped was an encouraging smile, but the thought that this girl might know something, have something to do with Ginger's death made her smile falter. "The sheriff told me that you had information about my cousin."

Tears filled the young girl's eyes. "I'm so sorry, so very sorry."

It was painful to watch this young girl look so miserable, sound so forlorn. Sylvie took Tanya's limp hand between hers. "What do you have to feel sorry about?"

"It was me. I didn't mean to." The tears continued. "But when I woke up, she was dead." Tanya slipped her hand from Sylvie's grasp and covered her face with both hands.

Hearing the sheriff inhale sharply, Sylvie felt as

though someone had just emptied a load of bricks onto her breastbone. She drew breath, but with difficulty. "Do you mean my cousin Ginger?"

The girl bent her knees and folded her arms around them. Then she began to rock back and forth, making the bed creak.

"Did you see my cousin?" Sylvie couldn't hold back the words. "She came to your store that first night she was in town, remember?"

"I didn't mean to. I was looking for…" The girl began to rock harder and faster.

Sylvie felt her heart beating faster. "What were you looking for?" The girl didn't answer her. Sylvie reached over to touch her, to reassure her.

The girl screamed, "Go away! I didn't mean to! It was an accident!"

Sylvie jerked her hand back. "What's wrong? How can I help you?"

Tanya screamed louder without words this time.

Sylvie leaped up from her chair, turning to the sheriff for help. Instead, he pulled her back toward the door.

The nurse came running into the room.

Sylvie took another step backward along with the sheriff.

The nurse tried to calm Tanya. But the girl only screamed louder, more frantically.

Another nurse rushed in. As she passed Sylvie, she said, "You'll have to leave now. Please."

Sylvie obeyed. Outside the door, she leaned back against the wall, breathing fast. She looked up into the sheriff's face. "Did you expect her to tell me that?"

He shook his head as he drew her down the hallway and out of the psych ward. "No, and I don't know what to make of it. I need to talk to her psychiatrist. Thank you for coming."

Sylvie felt his urgency to leave her and proceed with his investigation. So she merely nodded and let him go. But then she just stood outside the psych ward, trying to put it all together. She couldn't.

Ridge parked his SUV on the street in front of My Favorite Books. After the sheriff had found the lost girl, he'd called Ridge. The rest of what Keir told him, he still couldn't believe. But what did that matter? This development had been enough to cause Block to send Ridge north. And at this moment, that was all that mattered.

The front door to Sylvie's shop beckoned him. But now that he was here, he hesitated. Getting out of his vehicle, he reminded himself not to make the mistake of repeating a kiss or his ill-fated proposal.

He let himself into the brightly lit and inviting store. And there was Sylvie at her desk. She looked up at him and smiled with her whole face.

"I didn't expect you to come so soon," she said.

"The sheriff called my boss and he sent me

back." He had taken her hand and held it, unwilling to release her.

Something warm and wonderful expanded inside Sylvie. As she gazed into Ridge's eyes, she saw so much there meant for her and she read every line. Feeling the intensity between them, she slipped her hand from his and looked away. "Did the sheriff tell you that Tanya confessed to killing Ginger by accident?"

"Yes, but he also said that she was out of her mind on drugs." Ridge took another step toward her. "And you were right. They did find drugs in her room. Especially hallucinogenics. In particular LSD." He couldn't seem to stem the flow of words. "The hospital psychiatrist says that she is having frequent flashbacks from bad trips."

Recalling the scene with Tanya, Sylvie gripped the arms of her chair. "Yes, that's what Keir told me, too. But I was there. I visited her and I don't think we can dismiss her confession as unreliable as a result of her drug use. There may be some truth in her words."

Sylvie looked troubled. Hoping to make her feel better, he offered, "That's because you haven't confronted as many drug abusers as I have. They begin to lose touch with reality."

Rising, Sylvie took a step back from him. She wouldn't let him dismiss her opinion. "But why would Tanya say she'd killed Ginger by accident when she hadn't? Why would she run away? She was severely malnourished and suffered some frostbite. Something serious is going on with that girl and it's not just drugs. I feel it."

He pursued her. "Sylvie, we get false confessions all the time. And with someone like Tanya, who's been using hallucinogenics, the line between reality and drug-induced memories becomes blurred. She's not responsible for what she says. Or culpable."

She didn't give ground literally and figuratively. "I'm sorry, but I can't agree. I think Tanya knows something about Ginger's murder. There isn't any other reason for her to bring it up."

Her sweet fragrance drifted to him. She was standing so close. "Well, I'm going to talk to her myself tomorrow," he conceded.

"Good." She abruptly turned away from him.

Why was she withdrawing from him? It goaded him. He nearly proposed to her a second time. He clenched his teeth.

Sylvie turned back to him, but slowly. For a long moment, she stared into his eyes. She wished she had the courage to bring up his refused proposal. She wanted to say to him, "I have loved you for a long time, Ridge." But of course she couldn't say that.

The wall clock ticked loudly in the quiet room. He didn't know how long they stood there staring at each other. But then Sylvie brushed past him and headed to the small kitchen in the back.

As if they were connected by transparent fishing line, he followed her. "Sylvie…" he said, but then did not know how to go on. His heart seemed to be doing jumping jacks in his chest.

"I need to close up for the night," she said over her shoulder. He followed her into the small kitchen.

She was emptying the basket of used coffee grounds into the garbage. He wanted to say something to her. Somehow he needed to say something to her. But he could not put the confusion inside him into words. Besides, if he proposed, she would probably take him lightly again.

She turned to face him. She saw before her a good-looking man, more importantly a man who looked intelligent and commanding. But she wouldn't let him off the hook about his erstwhile proposal. "Ridge, how many women have you proposed to?"

Ridge froze in place. Why had she asked him that question? Had she read it in his face? Instantly the image of Ben's mother flashed through his mind. But for the first time in forever, it didn't taunt him. In fact, he only felt a sense of bittersweet loss. Sharon was dead. So what did it matter that she had married his best friend instead of him? It didn't matter. Not anymore. But he recognized also that the hesitance he'd felt about assuming responsibility for Ben had been related to leftover regret about Sharon choosing Ben's father over him. But no more.

Sylvie's voice intruded on his thoughts. "When I was a girl, Ridge, I had a crush on you. But now I have fallen in love with you for real."

Her honest words shocked him into replying, "If you love me, why didn't you just say yes, then?"

"Because you haven't realized yet or admitted why you proposed to me. And until you do, I will not say yes." She turned away again and began to wipe the kitchen counter and generally straighten up the kitchen, politely dismissing him.

For several moments, he stared at her back. He was tempted to once again reach out and grip her shoulders and try to understand her. But he felt incompetent.

Without a word, he turned and walked away. Outside, he felt the spring breeze against his heated face. He got into his SUV and sped off to his parents' house.

A few minutes later, Sylvie locked the door of her shop and then walked down the steps. She hadn't bothered to zip up her coat or put on her hat. Her hip hurt her today. The weather was changing and it always affected her.

Her mind took her back through all the times Ridge had touched or kissed her. Had those been what had given her the courage to tell Ridge the truth about her feelings? His actions had spoken loudly and she had told him how she felt. Still, he was denying his feelings for her and there was nothing she could do about it. And she wouldn't agree to any proposal from him until he was ready to be honest with both of them. Could she?

Or this might all be moot since he might not ask her to marry him again. This March could prove to be one of the worst months of her life. Her mood slid to the cold sidewalk. She stepped over it and walked on. Self-pity was not her style.

She crossed the street and walked down the side street toward the waterfront. The street was empty as usual. That would wonderfully change in another two months. This interminable winter would end. The crowds would come again and keep her too busy to mourn.

As she came abreast of the alley, she heard a man's voice. "Ms. Patterson?"

She halted. "Yes?"

It happened so fast she didn't have time to scream. A man whose face was hidden behind a snowmobiling mask lunged out from behind a short fir tree. He grabbed her. Pulled her behind the fir tree. He shoved a cloth in her face. It had a sickly sweet smell. Her knees weakened and blackness swallowed her.

# TWELVE

Later, Ridge stared out of the bedroom window at his parents' house. It was dark now and he saw only his own sorry reflection in the glass. He was restless. He felt as if he were on the brink of something, as though he were standing on tiptoe at the edge of a cliff.

His life in Madison had become predictable. But in Winfield nothing was predictable. This evening at the dinner table, both his mother and father had actually said a few words to him. And to each other.

But more upsetting, earlier he had purposely decided not to repeat his proposal to Sylvie but it had been a very difficult thing to do. He couldn't get her words out of his head. *I have fallen in love with you for real.*

His cell phone rang. He pulled it out of his pocket and flipped it open. "Matthews."

"Ridge, Sylvie hasn't come home," Milo said on the line. "Is she with you by some chance?"

Instantly alert, Ridge glanced at the bedside clock. "No, Milo, I left her at her store nearly two hours ago."

"Then I'm calling the sheriff. I've called everyone and no one has seen her."

Icy fear speared Ridge's heart. "Milo—" But before he could say anything further, Milo hung up. Ridge snapped his phone shut. As if experiencing an earthquake, he grabbed hold of the window sash. *Sylvie, where are you?*

Within the half hour, the sheriff entered the Matthewses' kitchen. Ridge had not gone out on his own to look for Sylvie though that had been his first impulse. But his professional knowledge had clicked into place. He needed to coordinate any search with the sheriff in order to be effective. Now he faced Keir, dread pulsing, jabbing him with each heartbeat. His parents stood silently behind him. "What's the plan?"

"I've issued an APB," Keir replied, thin-lipped. "I've called in everyone. I've notified the local radio and TV station and they will be alerting everyone that Sylvie is missing. Milo is faxing Sylvie's photograph to the TV station." The sheriff paused, exhaling loudly. "I don't think there's any possibility that this isn't related to Ginger's death. Do you?"

Ridge didn't bother to reply to this unnecessary question. "What can I do?"

"Follow me to headquarters." Keir was already turning toward the door. "All my deputies are going to meet up there and we will figure out who's going to be searching what area. And I have specific sites that I want to check for clues and to search."

"Like Leahy's place?" Ridge was snatching his coat off the peg by the door and shrugging it on.

Out of the blue, Ridge's dad spoke up. "You've heard the weather reports? A storm is headed our way. They don't know whether it will be rain or snow. Depends on the temp."

"I'm aware of that." Keir looked even grimmer. "Let's get going."

As Ridge turned to close the door behind him, his mother called after them, "Godspeed."

Sylvie came awake slowly as if someone was very gradually drawing back a curtain to the morning light. But this couldn't be morning, because there was no light. There was fabric over her eyes. And her wrists were bound together behind her. She was lying on a floor, a very cold floor. A musty smell of rotted wood filled her head and she moaned. Where was she?

"It's about time you came around." A man's harsh voice came from above her. He sounded irritated. "I didn't know how long the chloroform would knock you out. I must have left the rag on your face too long."

She turned her head toward the voice. Then she remembered. This must be the man—the one who had grabbed her. *Why am I here?* She tried to speak, but her mouth was too dry. She made only a croaking sound.

"Here, drink this." The man lifted her head and put a glass to her lips.

She didn't want to drink anything from him. But she had no choice. He held the back of her neck tightly and the strength in his hands frightened her. She took a sip. He squeezed her neck, silently insisting that she drink more. She drank several more swallows. Nearly gagging.

"Okay, that's enough. That should do it."

*Should do what?*

### March 26

The next morning, Ridge strode up the side of his parents' drive on his way inside. The long, fruitless night weighed him down. The skyline was gray and heavy with snow clouds, reflecting his mood. Overnight, the wild wind had changed direction. The stormy Low front had been blocked as it moved eastward by a stronger High stalled over the state of Michigan. This had forced its powerful winds to remain swirling over and gathering moisture from both Lake Michigan and Lake Superior. The saturated front was sweeping down from the northeast.

This was the perfect situation to bring snow down on their heads. He watched the tops of the tall trees sway this way and then the other way, bending against the whirling wind. He felt as though he were a victim of the same kind of confusion, as well. Where was Sylvie?

Every deputy in Winfield County had been searching all night long for Sylvie. He had been out, riding with Trish Lawson, following every road in their quadrant and trekking into isolated snowbound hunting shacks. All around the perimeter of the Chequamegon-Nicolet National Forest that occupied the center of the county.

Minutes ago, Trish had dropped him off at his vehicle parked in front of the sheriff's department. He'd come home to get some breakfast and change into dry shoes and his boots. Then he had an errand he had to do. No matter what the sheriff thought.

He opened the back door and walked into the kitchen and the fragrance of fresh-brewed coffee. His parents were sitting at the kitchen table, drinking coffee. His mother rose immediately and came to him. "Did they find her?"

He shook his head, rubbing one tired, twitching eye with the heel of his hand. "Not a sign of her. Deputies on loan from Ashland County are coming to take over the day shift and continue the search."

His dad put his coffee mug down. "Did you feel that wind? That bad front has moved in."

This was true on so many levels. Ridge nodded and sank down into the nearest chair, exhausted yet driven by his need to find Sylvie.

His mother went to the stove, dropped wheat bread into the toaster and quickly whipped up scrambled eggs for him. "When this snow starts, it will be the worst kind of lake-effect snow, wet and heavy."

His father got up and poured Ridge a mug of coffee and brought it back to the table, setting it in front of his son. "I've seen snow like that bend trees to the ground and break power lines. This is going to be bad."

Ridge clung to the warm mug of hot coffee. So many different feelings ricocheted in every direction within him, he tightened his self-control. "All that doesn't matter. We have to find her. We will find her." Ridge wondered if he was trying to convince his parents or himself.

Setting the plate of scrambled eggs and toast in front of him, his mother commented, "You're exhausted. You eat this and then maybe you can catch a few hours of sleep."

Ridge forced himself not to shovel in the warm breakfast. He needed this food and hot coffee to revive him. "I'm not going to bed. After I finish breakfast, I'm going to talk to that Tanya Hendricks at the hospital." That was his errand, the one the sheriff wouldn't approve of.

"You mean Ollie's granddaughter?" his mother asked.

Ridge nodded as he chewed buttered wheat toast. His eyes burned after hours and hours of searching, staring into darkness. "Sylvie spoke to Tanya yesterday. When I spoke to Sylvie late yesterday—" *Right before I took off and left her defenseless.* His gut twisted. "She told me that she had spoken to Tanya yesterday and that she thought the girl knew something about Ginger's murder."

"I heard that the girl confessed to killing Ginger accidentally. Do you think that might be true?" his dad asked.

"I don't know." Ridge took another long swallow of the hot brew. "But it is the lead I have to follow. And Sylvie said that the girl must have a reason for making a confession. And she's right." *Why didn't I listen to her? She was right. She was right about a lot of things.* Her words came again and again. *I have fallen in love with you for real.*

His dad pushed up from his chair. "You eat breakfast, then. I'm going to put chains onto your tires. If you're going to be driving around the county, you'll need them. The weatherman is predicting the end of the world."

Surprise rippled through Ridge again. His father hadn't made a joke like that for a very long time. And especially at a stressful time like this.

His mother sat down in the chair adjacent to Ridge. She bowed her head. He realized that she was praying. He masked his reaction to this by taking in large mouthfuls of scrambled eggs. *Whatever she is praying, Lord, double it. Please.*

He tightened his control again. He had much to do this day. With God's help.

Sylvie tried to think. But she couldn't. The thoughts in her mind fluttered around like lightning bugs, flickering in the pervasive darkness. His voice came again, louder and angrier. "Where was Ginger's hiding place? Where did she hide things?"

"Ginger?" she whispered.

"Yes, where did your cousin hide things?"

"My cousin?" she whispered again. Her mouth was so dry and her head seemed to be floating away.

He slapped her. "I don't want to hurt you. I didn't want to hurt your cousin. Now tell me. Where is her hiding place?"

Her cheek stinging, she tried to focus on his words. *Ginger's hiding place. Yes, she knew where Ginger's hiding place was.*

He shook her. "Tell me—"

Suddenly an old memory popped into place. She and Ginger, girls again, giggling and hiding love notes about boys in the… "In the ceiling. In the attic."

"Which attic?"

Her mind couldn't bring up the information he wanted…. "Attic?" she repeated.

He cursed. And then he slammed something against the floor and it broke right beside her head. She jumped. Was it wood? "Tell me!" he yelled. "Tell me! Or you've had it!"

\* \* \*

Ridge strode down the hallway to the psych ward. At the glassed-in partition, he halted and said, "I'm Ridge Matthews." He pulled out his state badge and showed it the nurse. "I'm here to see Tanya Hendricks."

"I don't know whether she can have visitors," the nurse hedged.

"I'm not a visitor. I'm a law officer and I need to talk with her concerning a kidnapping and murder."

"Our psychiatrist is on the floor," she said, rising from her chair. "I'll go get him."

"You do that." Ridge felt his patience slipping from his fingers.

The psychiatrist came to the window and after a few moments of discussion, he pressed the button to let Ridge in. "I want to be present as you question her," the psychiatrist said. "She's been quite agitated. And I don't want to trigger any more flashbacks. Stress can often do that."

"No problem. But I want you to understand that she may have information which will lead us to Sylvie Patterson. I don't have time to waste."

"That's why I'm letting you in." He nodded, gesturing toward her hallway. "I realize that time is of the essence. But Tanya's grasp of reality is very tenuous at this moment. I must protect her, also, no matter what the court order said."

"Got it." Ridge followed the psychiatrist into

Tanya's room. The girl's half-eaten breakfast sat on her bed table, which had been pushed to the side. She was pale and disheveled. And she was lying limply, staring vacantly at the ceiling.

In contrast, Ridge felt as if he were a motor set on high idle. "Miss Hendricks," Ridge addressed her, keeping his tone even, "I need to talk to you about something very important. I need your help."

"I want to tell the truth, all of it. I can't carry it all inside me anymore. It makes me…feel sick." The girl shivered once very hard.

He took out a small handheld tape recorder. "I will be tape-recording this." He repeated the Miranda to her just to be on the safe side and asked her if she understood it.

The girl looked at him then and she nodded, pressing a hand control. The bed hummed as it elevated her head and shoulders. "I know you," she said, adjusting to the sitting position. "You were with the sheriff when he questioned me and you were there when Jim robbed Ollie's store."

This news stiffened Ridge's spine. He approached her. The psychiatrist hung back just inside the door, leaning against the wall. "Jim? You mean it was Jim Leahy, your stepfather, who robbed Ollie's?"

"Yes, it was Jim. I recognized him even though he had the mask on. I mean, I know his voice. That's why I didn't give him the money right away. I was so shocked." She spoke without emphasis, stringing words together. "And then you were chasing him. And I didn't want you to catch him. So I ran after you. I picked up a stick and I hit you over the head with it. It was a big stick, almost as thick as a log. You didn't hear me running after you."

Ridge sat down in the bedside chair. Abruptly. "Why did you hit me?" Ridge kept his voice very calm. But the back of his head tingled where he had been struck. "Why didn't you let me catch him?"

"He was my supplier. If you caught him, I wouldn't get any more stuff."

"I see. That makes sense." Ridge's hands curled into fists. "Sylvie Patterson visited you Friday. Do you know that she has been kidnapped?"

"Yes, I saw it on the TV news. Jim must have kidnapped her." The girl's voice was serene, flat.

"Jim?" Ridge's fists tightened. "Why would he kidnap Sylvie?"

"Because she's his last chance. He has to get that money." Now her voice picked up a slight momentum. "He didn't find it in any of those houses or apartments. Not in that dead girl's apartment. Or the bookshop. Or in that house, that house that belonged to Ginger's mom, Shirley. She's nice."

"What money?" Ridge moved to the edge of his chair.

"The money from the winning lottery ticket. My grandpa was so mad because he knew someone had bought a winning lottery ticket at his store last fall.

But they never turned it in. So he didn't get his percentage of the winnings. He said he could have retired and lived well for the rest of his life on it."

Thoughts bursting like popcorn in his mind, Ridge forced himself to just sit quietly and let it all come out. Any questions from him might stem the flow.

"Then that girl, that Ginger, stopped at the store and told me that she had bought the winning lottery ticket last fall. But she hadn't known it. Because she was away, in Alaska, I think it was. Anyway, she read it in a newspaper in Superior on her way home. So she came in all happy and said that she had all her lottery tickets from last year in a hiding place and that she would come back in tomorrow. She'd come to Ollie's the next morning and turn it in. And she'd be a millionaire. But then she couldn't, because she died."

All this was said in a singsong voice, but the quickening tempo showed the girl's stress rising. Could he believe her? Could Ginger's murder and every break-in have been caused by that winning lottery ticket that had never been turned in? It was ridiculous. Outlandish. But it all made sense. Someone had been looking for something. Something worth killing for. And a lottery ticket worth millions could cause all of that. He finally had the motive.

The flow had stopped. He must prime the pump. Again, he kept his voice even as he asked, "Tanya, did Jim kill Ginger?"

Tanya folded her arms around her knees and started rocking back and forth. "I wanted that money. Then I could leave this awful little town. And then I could have my life back. I don't like being poor. Mom said she'd send me money. But I would have to wait. She said my new stepfather would send me to college."

She rocked harder. "She'd persuade him. I just had to wait. But I haven't heard from her for a long time now. Maybe my new stepfather hasn't agreed to give her the money. Or maybe she doesn't want to share it with me. So I'm stuck in this awful place. I mean, my grandpa is okay, but…this isn't my life."

The psychiatrist walked farther into the room and rested a hand on Ridge's shoulder, silently asking for restraint.

Ridge nodded. "I'm sorry that you haven't heard from your mother. But did Jim kill Ginger?"

Tanya looked him right in the eye and ceased rocking. "I went there to see if I could find the winning ticket. That girl told me she would be out all night with her cousin, that Sylvie who came to see me. I remember crawling in through a window." She began rocking again. "And I was pulling books from the shelves, and then I had a flashback, you know, a bad trip. When I woke up, I was lying at the bottom of the steps on top of her."

Tanya began rocking very fast, very hard. "I don't know what happened." Her voice rose, shrill, frantic. "Maybe she came in and I was having a flashback and we might have struggled together and then fallen down the stairs. I was at the bottom of the stairs on top of her when I woke up but I can't remember…but Jim must've been there, too." She moaned and bent her forehead to her folded knees.

Watching this young girl distressed him. She shouldn't be here. In this condition. In his mind, he pictured the girl's mother as he had known her in high school. Right now he wished that she were here so he could tell her what he thought of her mothering skills. "But…did you tell Jim? Tell him you knew he was after the lottery ticket?"

"No, but I know Jim was at the convenience store that night," Tanya said. "He'd just bought some liquor and was walking out the back door when that Ginger, that girl from Alaska, came and started blabbing about the winning ticket. Why did she tell us? Why would she blab about it to a stranger like that?"

*Because she was an honest person and honest people don't think like dishonest people.* Ridge coaxed her to go on. "Tanya, where would Jim take Sylvie? We've searched his house. But she wasn't there and neither was he."

Tanya stared at the ceiling, her eyes wide. "There's a place…a place south, it's where he picks up drugs. It's an old bar…it's been closed up for years. Behind it, his supplier brings the stuff. Jim took me with him once. Because I was bugging him. And he had to go."

Again, she looked directly into Ridge's eyes. "Jim's not a bad guy. But he lost all his money. Bad investments. And they're about to foreclose on his place here. My mom left him. He started gambling. And he owes some really scary people a lot of money. A lot. He had to have it. He's not a bad guy. Really."

The psychiatrist squeezed Ridge's shoulder hard. Ridge understood. He rose and offered his hand to Tanya. "Thank you, you've helped me. Now we can find Sylvie."

She let him press her hand once. "I'm sorry I hit you. I didn't mean to hurt you."

"I know. Get better now." Ridge turned and walked out the door, leaving the psychiatrist to deal with the sad, abandoned girl.

He nearly ran to the elevator, and on the first floor, he hurried out the door nearest the parking lot, his boots slapping through about three inches of sloppy wet snow. He flipped open his phone and speed-dialed the sheriff. Wet snow splashed him in the face and the wind roared around the building, pounding, beating him. Unlocking his door, he climbed inside and slammed it against the wind.

Keir came on the line. Ridge interrupted him, "I know where Sylvie is. You know that abandoned bar on the highway halfway between Washburn and Ashford? Tanya told me. She also said Ginger was killed because of a lottery ticket. But she thinks

Jim's taken Sylvie to that old bar. I'm going there now. Meet me."

The sheriff barked questions, but Ridge couldn't waste time on that. "I'm heading there now. Meet me." He started the SUV and roared out of his parking spot. The fierce wind buffeted the vehicle as if it were a mere paper boat on a windswept stream. Set on high speed, Ridge's windshield wipers batted at the pelting snow, sliding over his windshield.

Ridge's pulse kept pace with the wind. The fear that Jim might accidentally kill someone again, kill Sylvie, set his teeth on edge. *A nice guy. Yeah, right.*

Sylvie hated this fuzzy, awful feeling.

"I'm going to leave you now," the man above her said. "I didn't mean to hurt you. I'll go to the hiding place and get what I need. And then when I can, I'll call and tell them where you are—"

Then Sylvie heard the door open hard, then footsteps, coming toward her, vibrating on the floor, not leaving. A rush of cold, wet air along the floor made her shiver. The man standing above her turned; she could hear the soles of his shoes grate on the gritty floor beside her head. Had help come?

"Why did you bring him along?" the man standing above her asked, sounding shrill and worried.

"Because *he's* tired of waiting for the money," another voice, low and menacing, replied.

Sylvie was glad that this person wasn't speaking to her. He didn't sound like a man who would take no for an answer.

"I've got two more days," the man who'd brought her here objected, sounding even more shrill.

"Well, things change," the low, menacing voice replied. "And anyway, how are you going to come up with numbers like that in two days? And I was in the neighborhood. I won't need to make a special trip."

"Now, wait a minute. I've just got information that I've needed, that I've been looking for! I'll have the money in two days for him."

Another male voice asked, "Who's the chick on the floor?"

"Don't bother about her. She hasn't heard or seen anything. She won't be able to testify against me."

"You brought her here?" the low, menacing voice asked him. "Why?"

"She had the information I needed."

Sylvie wondered why a childhood hiding place was so important to this man and what money he he talking about.

"So," the menacing voice said, "I have to take care of two of you."

"No!" The man who had brought her objected, sounding panicked. "She doesn't know anything. And I told you—"

The sound of sirens buffeted Sylvie's hypersensitive hearing. She stiffened where she lay. Would they kill her? *Dear Father! Save me!*

A gun exploded above Sylvie. She screamed. A heavy weight fell across her middle. She screamed again. Footsteps ran away.

# THIRTEEN

In his SUV parked behind a clump of trees, Ridge heard first the siren and then the gunshot from inside the derelict bar. Inside, someone had heard the siren, too. Someone who had a gun. Who was the idiot who was arriving at a hostage situation with siren blaring? It forced his hand. He'd been waiting for backup. Now Ridge jumped out of his SUV. The wind wailed around him. He slid on the wet, sloppy snow. Sylvie was inside. Sylvie might be…

He charged toward the door. One good kick and the hinges. gave way from the rotted wood. He wrenched off two boards that had been nailed across the doorway. "Police!" he bellowed.

He halted inside, instinctively seeking shelter in the shadows, getting his bearings in the darkened building. As his eyes adjusted, he looked across the room and saw that the room was empty. Or was it? Then more gunshots came from outside behind the tavern. Backup must have arrived.

\* \* \*

Sylvie heard more gunshots. But from farther away. From outside. She panted, straining to breathe against the weight compressing her diaphragm. Still, she was afraid to move. Something too horrible to name was wetting her body from the soft but heavy thing that lay over her. She didn't want to think, wouldn't let herself think what it was. But it made it so hard to breathe. She tried to roll it off but was still hampered by having her hands tied behind her.

More sirens. Noise. Shouts. Sylvie steeled herself. She began praying the only scripture that came to her, the Twenty-third Psalm.

"Sylvie!" Ridge's voice came to her through the darkness.

"I'm here, Ridge!" she shouted. "I'm here. Help me. Oh, please."

She felt his footsteps vibrate the floor as he ran to her. The weight was rolled off her. The blindfold was ripped off her head and she looked up into Ridge's eyes. "Oh, Ridge, Ridge."

He untied her numb hands and, lifting her off the floor, he laid her on what must have once been a bar. There was almost no daylight. But from above, snowflakes sifted down onto her face. The pins-and-needles sensation flared in her hands that had been bound. She gasped with the pain of it.

"Are you hurt? You look like you're bleeding."

Ridge ran his hands lightly over her as if searching for injuries.

"I'm fine." She tried to remember, to bring up the words the man who'd kidnapped her had said. "Ridge. Is he dead?"

"I don't know. Can you sit up?"

"No. Everything hurts, aches. I'm pins and needles all over."

"Lie still. I'll be right back. I have to check him."

After that, everything became a blur. Everything except the fact that she was in Ridge's arms. And, as she knew she had been all night, in God's arms.

Hours later, Ridge insisted on carrying her, wrapped in a blanket, up the steps to the Patterson apartment. She'd insisted on going home from the hospital, but would go in to her doctor for a visit in the morning. At the door, Milo and Ben greeted them. For a few moments, there were only hugs and tears. Ridge laid Sylvie on the sofa in the living room. She gazed out the large windows at the dark sky. The wind still slapped against the glass, dashing ice particles against it. But the snow had stopped. The eye of the storm had moved on.

Sylvie was wearing fresh, faded green scrubs that had been given to her at the hospital. The clothing Sylvie had been wearing had been taken as evidence. She'd taken a shower at the hospital and also given a blood sample to tell if there was any evidence of drugs in her system. She sighed, a great contentment stealing over her. "I feel like I've been to China and back again twice."

"We were worried," Ben admitted. "Real worried."

Milo stood beside the young boy and put an arm around his shoulder. "Yes, we were. But everything is all right now. Come on, Ben. Let's go in the kitchen and warm up the pot of soup from yesterday. Sylvie looks like she could use a bowl and so does Ridge." Milo shepherded the young boy out to the kitchen and closed the door behind them.

Ridge gently lifted Sylvie's head and shoulders and sat down as her pillow. He stroked her hair back from her face, upset by the few scratches and scrapes on her cheeks and forehead. Again, the fear of losing her welled up inside of him. It must've shown on his face because Sylvie whispered, "It's all right, Ridge. I'm all right."

"I should be comforting you." His rough voice scoured his throat. *I almost lost her.*

She reached up and stroked his cheek, just as she did that day in her kitchen in the back of her shop. But the effect was even more powerful now. Would the unnerving image of Jim Leahy's dead body lying on top of Sylvie ever be blotted from his mind?

"It's really all over then, right?" she asked.

"Yes, the two suspects who have priors on drug trafficking were caught at the bar and are in custody," Ridge said, but he continued to stroke her hair back from her face, her beautiful face. *I'll never get tired of looking at you, Sylvie. Never.*

"It's just so bizarre." Sylvie sighed. "It was all about a lottery ticket. I didn't even know that Ginger bought lottery tickets."

Her light blond hair glimmered in the dimly lit room. The shadows cast from the lamplight outlined the fine bones of her face. "I guess it was her secret vice. I'm still having trouble putting it all together in my mind."

With his palm, he smoothed out the worry lines from her forehead. "I know what you mean, but as soon as Tanya told me about the lottery ticket, everything snapped into focus," Ridge said. Nothing could disrupt the deep peace he felt with Sylvie so near, not even a discussion of murder. "That lottery ticket was the missing clue. The motive that explained the break-ins and Ginger's death."

"Tell me again." She stroked his cheek again, her eyes probing his. "I'm having trouble keeping it all straight."

He kissed her palm and then, lifting her shoulders, bent to press a kiss on her forehead. He lowered her back to his lap. "According to Tanya, Ginger stopped—that first night back in town—at Ollie's convenience store probably to pick up those groceries we found in her refrigerator. Somehow Ginger had found out that she had purchased the winning numbers on a lottery ticket that was due to expire on the twenty-eighth of this month. I think Tanya said Ginger read a newspaper on the way home."

"I've read stories like that. Stories about lottery tickets that are about to expire but that no one has claimed," Sylvie murmured, turning her body slightly more toward Ridge.

Cradling her hand in his, Ridge nodded. "Ginger couldn't resist telling Tanya about it. After all, she had bought the ticket at Ollie's."

Sylvie's eyes closed. "I can see Ginger doing that. I can see her bubbling over with the news. That was the big wow surprise she had for me." Her voice cracked on "surprise."

Ridge grunted in agreement and stroked her palm, the soft mound below her thumb with his. "But unfortunately she told Tanya and indirectly Jim Leahy, who was about to go out the rear entrance, that she would be out all evening with you. And that the ticket was in her hiding place."

"Do you think that they went together? To search for the ticket?" She rubbed her cheek against his hand. He read in her face that she was experiencing the same pull to touch him as he felt for her.

"From what Tanya said, I take it that she went alone and began ransacking the apartment and then had a bad LSD flashback."

Sylvie laced her fingers into his hair and, lifting

her head, pulled his lips down to meet hers—once—lightly. She inhaled, laying her head back down.

Ridge continued, "Your cousin must have come home during her search. They might have struggled. But I don't think that Tanya killed her."

"I think Jim must've done it. He told me...he told me he hadn't wanted to hurt my cousin. But Ginger would have fought him. She was feisty like that." Sylvie's face twisted in pain.

Ridge kissed her again, and smoothed his hand over her face. If only he could pluck these hard memories from her mind. He fingered her silky hair again. "Anyway, neither of them found the ticket." *And Leahy left Tanya to think that she had killed Ginger. Yeah, a real nice guy.* Ridge found himself clenching his jaw and made himself relax.

Sylvie turned her face toward him again and began to sit up, moving against him. "Why did they take the computers? Ginger's laptop and my PC?"

Ridge shook his head. "Maybe to pawn. Or maybe they just wanted to use them. They haven't searched Leahy's place thoroughly yet."

The phone rang in the other room. Ridge hoped it would be nothing that would disturb his sitting here, holding Sylvie and stroking her hair. He would be happy to stay like this for the rest of his life.

The door to the kitchen opened. Milo held the phone receiver in his hand. "I'm so sorry to bother you two, but it's Ollie. He apologized for calling.

It's about that winning lottery ticket. If we could find it today and turn it in, it would mean a lot of money for him. It has to be turned in no later than midnight or it expires."

Sylvie had no choice. She sat up completely and pushed her hair back from her face. "Tell him—"

Ridge interrupted her. "Do you know where Ginger's hiding place is?"

Sylvie nodded wearily. Suddenly chilled, she leaned against Ridge, seeking his warmth. "Yes, it just came to me again. I remembered it when Jim threatened me. I think it's at her apartment over my shop."

"But we've asked you over and over if you knew of any hiding places in any of the homes that have been broken into," Ridge objected.

"It just came to me when Jim was questioning me…." She leaned her head into the crook of his neck, feeling the stubble on his chin rasp her cheek. "It was like a lightbulb going on in my head. I'd forgotten it. We were just kids the last time Ginger used that hiding place or at least I thought it had been way over ten years. Do you think that drug might have helped me remember?"

Milo spoke up, "No. Maybe you weren't supposed to remember until now."

Her father's words moved her to action. "I'll get some socks and shoes on and then we can go over to the apartment." Sylvie pushed herself up from the couch, leaving Ridge's warmth, and limped toward her bedroom.

Ridge followed her. "Are you sure you're up to doing this?"

She pulled open her sock drawer and began rummaging in it for a warm pair. "I'll have to be, won't I? Ollie is a good man. And he has Tanya to take care of, too. The bad shape she's in, she will need a lot of help to get better. And that kind of help is really pricey." She found a pair of wool socks and shut the drawer.

Ridge turned her away from the dresser and wrapped his arms around her, holding her very close. "I hope you realize that I never intend to let you go."

She felt his lips move against her ear. The contact electrified her.

"I love you, Sylvie. Will you marry me?"

"You love me?" She looked up into his dark eyes, which gazed into hers directly and honestly. She read them with ease.

"I love you deeply. And completely. I understand that now. I understand how much now." He kissed her forehead. "You were right to refuse my proposal. I had been living so many years just to do my job that I had forgotten how to feel like a person, like a man in love. But when I thought I might lose you, everything became very clear in my mind. Does that make sense?"

She believed him and smiled. They'd come through this trial together. "No more marriage of convenience?" She ran her finger down the bridge of his nose, teasing him.

He didn't answer her with words, but with a kiss that left her limp in his arms.

She kissed him once in return—just to be polite. She chuckled silently and then said, "I'll marry you, Ridge. Now help me find my shoes." She rubbed noses with him.

He chuckled aloud, suddenly feeling lighter, more buoyant than he had for years.

Sylvie sat on the end of her bed and began pulling on thick wool socks. Ridge went to her closet and picked up the first pair of shoes he saw, a pair of purple high heels. "How about these?"

She threw her pillow at him and then they were both laughing. And kissing.

After a short drive, Sylvie and Ridge walked up the snowy, wet path to the rear entrance of Sylvie's shop.

Ollie was there waiting for them, his collar turned up against the wind. "I really appreciate this, Sylvie. I'm so sorry to bother you after all you've been through in the last twenty-four hours." Words poured from the normally taciturn man. "I heard about Ginger buying the winning lottery ticket last fall. I can't help feeling guilty about this. But I get a lot of business selling lottery tickets. And if I didn't sell them, people would just go elsewhere to buy them."

Sylvie unlocked the door and switched on the

lights. "None of this is your fault, Ollie. No one forced Ginger to buy that lottery ticket. And no one forced Jim Leahy to try to steal it." She left unsaid: *Or your granddaughter Tanya.*

Trying to blot out the memory of finding Ginger's body here, she averted her eyes as she led the two men inside and up the stairs. There, she pointed upward at the ceiling. "Ridge, would you pull down that trap door." He did as she asked. And then she climbed up the narrow steps that had come down with the trap door. Light shone from below, illuminating the attic where most of Ginger's things remained. Sylvie asked herself the question again—why hadn't the old hiding place occurred to her when she was here with her father? The only answer was that she must have been too upset, grieving and too confused to think of it then.

Stooped over, she went to one of the boards in the old plank ceiling and pushed on it. It slid about two inches. Down fluttered many, many lottery tickets. Sylvie reached into the small space to make sure that she had gotten every one and found a couple more lottery tickets wedged in a crack. When the cleverly constructed cubbyhole was completely bare, she scooped them all up and carried them down the steps to the small kitchen table. "It wasn't just one." She spread them out to be inspected. Ridge hovered at her elbow, his concern for her palpable.

"I brought the winning numbers with me," Ollie said, pulling a slip of paper from his breast pocket and reading off the numbers.

Sylvie looked at one of the tickets still in her hand and said with a jolt of surprise, "I have it here."

"So do I." Ridge had picked up another ticket and now waved it.

Sylvie glanced at the ticket, leaning against his arm and then looked at the others. "Ginger must have played the same numbers over and over."

"A lot of people do that," Ollie said. "That must have been how she knew she won. She read about the uncollected prize and recognized the numbers as the ones she always played."

"What is the date we're looking for, Ollie?" Ridge asked.

"October 27 of last year."

The three of them quickly searched through the many tickets. Sylvie stayed close to Ridge. His presence gave her the strength to deal with this heartbreaking chore.

"Here it is," Ridge said, holding out the lottery ticket to Ollie. "This one is dated October 27."

Ollie let out a whoop and snatched the ticket from Ridge's hand.

"Just a minute," Ridge cautioned. "I don't think it has all those numbers. Check it."

Ollie cursed softly. "Sorry about that, Sylvie, but he is right. The 03 is wrong."

"Let's see if she bought two that day," Ridge suggested.

The three of them quickly went through the remaining tickets. No luck. Sylvie rested her head on Ridge's shoulder. "Ginger only bought that one ticket on October 27," Sylvie said. "Just like every other day she was in Winfield last year." *All for nothing.*

"But that can't be," Ollie declared. "I know that my store sold a ticket with those numbers, evidently the numbers Ginger always played, on October 27 of last year."

"I'm afraid," Ridge said, putting into words what she'd just realized—the awful, ironic truth, "that the winning ticket was sold to someone other than Ginger. Whoever entered Ginger's numbers on this ticket on October 27 made one mistake, entered one number wrong. And it's just as you decided before. Somebody bought the winning ticket and either it's sitting buried in someone's wallet or it hit the trash when they got home from vacation."

Ollie crumpled the useless ticket and threw it on the table. "Worthless!"

*One very important mistake. One life-and-death error.* Sylvie pressed her face against Ridge's chest for support. Two people had lost their lives. And the ticket was of no value.

# EPILOGUE

*May 25*

Lilacs in various vases composed the centerpiece on the refreshment table near the kitchen. Their fragrance filled the church basement. Dressed in a lavender floral skirt and blouse, Sylvie gazed around the circle of women sitting on folding chairs. On one side of her sat her future mother-in-law, Ellen Matthews. On her other side sat her aunt Shirley and Rae-Jean on the next chair and on her lap her baby. Under the fluorescent lights, the room was filled with cheerful feminine chatter.

Trish Lawson, who was just beginning to show with her first pregnancy, carried over to Sylvie another large white-and-silver wrapped bridal shower gift from the table that had been piled high with gifts. Sylvie had this gift to open and then Audra Harding would cut the white sheet cake that she had baked and artfully decorated for the shower.

Sylvie carefully undid the wrapping but still managed to break one ribbon. She tried to look upset, but today she could only smile.

"Ha!" Florence Lévesque exclaimed. "That's the fifth ribbon you've broken. That means you and Ridge will have five children."

"I broke six ribbons at my shower last fall," Audra announced, "and look what happened to me!" She patted her very prominent middle. "Twins!"

"Well, that's certainly an efficient way to have seven children. Only two more pregnancies to go," Florence piped up. General laughter followed this announcement.

Beside her, her future mother-in-law smiled. The change in Ellen Matthews over the past two months was just short of amazing. Sylvie had dreaded the moment Ridge and she told his parents of their plans to marry in June. Sylvie had thought that they would be against the marriage. And she had shrunk from their rejection and worried how it would hurt Ridge. But both Ellen and Marv Matthews had accepted the news and had, bit by bit, started coming back to life.

"Well," Sylvie spoke up, "we are planning on me having my hip surgery this fall. Babies will just have to wait until I have healed from that."

The women in the circle nodded and smiled. They didn't have to voice their happiness. Sylvie read joy on every face. The only slight regret, and it was very slight, was that Sylvie would be moving away to Madison with Ridge. His crucial work as a state homicide detective must go on. Sylvie and Ridge had been visiting small towns near Madison, looking for a home to buy. Sylvie wanted to settle in a smaller community, which she could become an active part of, especially since Ridge's work would take him from home often. And she was used to small-town living. She wanted to be in a community where she knew everyone's name.

"Oh, how lovely," Sylvie said sincerely, lifting out an intricately crocheted afghan, done tastefully in different shades of white. "Did you make this, Elsie?"

Elsie Ryerson, who sat beside Trish, nodded and smiled. "I didn't know if these old hands—" Elsie lifted up her arthritic hands "—could do it. But they did."

"It's lovely and it will go with whatever colors we decide on. Thank you." Sylvie carefully folded the attractive afghan back into the box.

Then she heard male voices and the shuffling of feet coming down the steps into the church basement. One by one entered Keir Harding, Grey Lawson, Chaney Franklin, Tom Robson with Chad Keski at his side, and bringing up the rear were Marv Matthews, Milo, Ben and finally her Ridge. Sylvie felt herself blush.

Florence Lévesque greeted the men with the news that Sylvie and Ridge were destined to have at least five children. The men took this in good part, nodding and laughing. Then Ridge said, "Keir let it slip that his wife made the cake—"

"So we decided we had to come and investigate," Grey Lawson added. "See if it's up to her usual standards."

"You bet," Tom added and Marv nodded in agreement.

"And of course we were considering your waistlines," Chaney teased. "If we eat more cake, you'll eat less."

Rae-Jean hopped up from her chair and scolded with a smile, "Waistlines! There's nothing wrong with our waistlines." She and her daughter still lived with Shirley and Tom, but everyone still had hopes that she would finally agree to counseling with Chaney.

"Enough of this nonsense," Milo said sensibly. "We want cake."

"Sounds like a plan, a delicious one," Tom added.

Many of the church ladies still scolded the men good-naturedly. But of course, the men would be given cake, too. After all, they had to carry all the gifts upstairs and stow them into the waiting vehicle—strenuous labor to be sure.

Sylvie's gifts would be stored in the attic of Ginger's apartment where Sylvie had found the worthless lottery ticket that had cost two lives. The gifts would stay there until Ridge and she were married in June and had returned from their honeymoon. Then they could take the gifts to their new home.

A moment of sadness dampened Sylvie's buoyant spirits. The funeral luncheon for Ginger had taken place in this room only three months before. *Ginger, I still miss you. I wish you could be here. But I know that I will see you again in God's time. And Tanya is out of the hospital and rehab, and is doing better. Her mother sent money for Tanya's treatment, but hasn't come to visit. Why do people do things like that?*

Then Sylvie watched as Audra, with her daughter, Evie, at her side went to cut the cake. Keir hurried to join them. He put his arm around Audra and kissed her cheek and then lifted up Evie for a hug. Trish slipped over to stand beside her husband, Grey, who tucked her close to his side. Tom with Chad gravitated to Shirley and Marv to Ellen. Ridge, Milo and Ben came to stand around Sylvie.

Ben looked happy. After speaking to a county social worker and psychologist, Sylvie and Ridge had decided to let Milo adopt Ben. The social worker and psychologist had urged this since they believed that Ben had bonded with Milo and with the community of Winfield. They did not advise taking Ben to the Madison area, one more disruption in his young life. And everyone hoped that Doyle Keski's parental rights to Chad would be terminated after Doyle had been convicted of holding up Bugsy's. The stolen money in the paper bag had been found in Doyle's truck's wheel well. Then, Tom and Shirley would begin the adoption process to gain Chad as their son.

Sylvie was at peace with Ben becoming her younger brother. Ben had been delighted when Milo had asked if he would like to be his son. And Sylvie did not feel so bad about leaving her father since he wouldn't be alone. And after all, Madison wasn't that far away.

Standing behind Sylvie, Ridge rested his hands on her shoulders, his usual way of connecting with her. She reached up, took one and pressed it to her cheek. *I love you, Ridge. Forever. Amen.*

\* \* \* \* \*

*In 2008, look for Lyn Cote's new historical series featuring three Quaker sisters who are strong enough to face any challenge God puts before them.*

*Visit www.eHarlequin.com or www.LynCote.net to check for this future series.*

Dear Reader,

So we come to the end of another series, HARBOR INTRIGUE. I've written three stories about three heroes and three heroines. I hope that their stories have uplifted and satisfied you as well as intrigued you. Very soon I will begin writing my next series, which will be for the new Love Inspired Historical line. I enjoy writing contemporary romantic suspense, but I love to write historicals. My new series begins the year after the Civil War. Three Quaker sisters each have a different challenge to face and conquer, and each brave heroine will attract one special man. I hope you will look for this new line of books, which will debut in 2008. Please e-mail me at l.cote@juno.com or visit my Web site www.LynCote.net and leave me a message there.

Lyn Cote

## QUESTIONS FOR DISCUSSION

1. Did you feel sorry for anyone in the story? Who? And why?

2. Ridge's parents had suffered a great loss. Why do you think they reacted in the way they did? How would you have reacted?

3. Why did Ridge feel uncomfortable around Ben? Do you think they made the right decision letting Milo adopt Ben?

4. Why do you think Chaney did not want to know the results of the paternity test? Do you think he was right or wrong? Why?

5. Why do you think it was so hard for Ridge to express or even acknowledge his love for Sylvie?

6. Do you approve of lotteries? Why or why not?

7. Why do you think people start taking drugs? What do you think is the best strategy for stopping this destructive trend?

8. What would you do if you were gifted with several million dollars?

9. What problems do you think you would encounter in this situation?

10. Have you ever witnessed or heard of any acts of ecoterrorism? If so, explain.

# *Love Inspired*®

Celebrate Love Inspired's 10th anniversary
with top authors and great stories all year long!

## A Tiny Blessings Tale

**Don't judge a person
by appearance alone.**

Life on the mission field
had given Eric a passion
for finding homes for
the world's abandoned
children, but when he
falls for a beautiful model,
will she be able to share
his vision?

**Look for**

# MISSIONARY
# DADDY
## BY
# LINDA
# GOODNIGHT

*Available in August
wherever you buy books.*

LIMD0707

Steeple
Hill®

**www.SteepleHill.com**

# REQUEST YOUR FREE BOOKS!

## 2 FREE RIVETING INSPIRATIONAL NOVELS PLUS 2 FREE MYSTERY GIFTS

*Love Inspired®*
# SUSPENSE

**YES!** Please send me 2 FREE Love Inspired® Suspense novels and my 2 FREE mystery gifts. After receiving them, if I don't wish to receive any more books, I can return the shipping statement marked "cancel." If I don't cancel, I will receive 4 brand-new novels every month and be billed just $3.99 per book in the U.S. or $4.74 per book in Canada, plus 25¢ shipping and handling per book and applicable taxes, if any*. That's a savings of 20% off the cover price! I understand that accepting the 2 free books and gifts places me under no obligation to buy anything. I can always return a shipment and cancel at any time. Even if I never buy another book from Steeple Hill, the two free books and gifts are mine to keep forever.

123 IDN EL5H   323 IDN ELQH

| | | |
|---|---|---|
| Name | (PLEASE PRINT) | |
| Address | | Apt. # |
| City | State/Prov. | Zip/Postal Code |

Signature (if under 18, a parent or guardian must sign)

### Order online at www.LoveInspiredSuspense.com

### Or mail to Steeple Hill Reader Service™:

**IN U.S.A.:** P.O. Box 1867, Buffalo, NY 14240-1867
**IN CANADA:** P.O. Box 609, Fort Erie, Ontario L2A 5X3

Not valid to current Love Inspired Suspense subscribers.

### Want to try two free books from another series?
### Call 1-800-873-8635 or visit www.morefreebooks.com

* Terms and prices subject to change without notice. NY residents add applicable sales tax. Canadian residents will be charged applicable provincial taxes and GST. This offer is limited to one order per household. All orders subject to approval. Credit or debit balances in a customer's account(s) may be offset by any other outstanding balance owed by or to the customer. Please allow 4 to 6 weeks for delivery.

**Your Privacy:** Steeple Hill is committed to protecting your privacy. Our Privacy Policy is available online at www.eHarlequin.com or upon request from the Reader Service. From time to time we make our lists of customers available to reputable firms who may have a product or service of interest to you. If you would prefer we not share your name and address, please check here. ☐

LISUS07

# *Love Inspired®*
# SUSPENSE

## TITLES AVAILABLE NEXT MONTH

### Don't miss these four stories in August

### MURDER BY MUSHROOM by Virginia Smith
*Cozy mystery*

At the church potluck, Jackie Hoffner's casserole *killed*—literally, unfortunately for the late Mrs. Farmer. Caught in the police searchlights, Jackie would have to rely on handsome Trooper Dennis Walsh and some snooping church ladies to uncover who had cooked up the scheme to frame her.

### CAUGHT REDHANDED by Gayle Roper

When Merry Kramer discovered a body while on her morning jog, she wondered whether danger would ever stop following her. She thought she knew the killer, but if she was unable to *prove* what she had found out, was it worth risking her life or losing her wonderful fiancé?

### HIDE IN PLAIN SIGHT by Marta Perry
*The Three Sisters Inn*

The Amish countryside may have been a peaceful escape to craftsman Cal Burke, but returning city girl Andrea Hampton felt only its bitter memories. Family secrets, once bound tight, began unraveling with an attack on her sister and with the neighbors' new hostility. Relying on Cal, Andrea had to get to the truth quickly—her life depended on it.

### SCARED TO DEATH by Debby Giusti

A frantic call from a dying friend left Kate Murphy embroiled in a sinister black-market deal and in danger of sharing her friend's fate. Widower Nolan Price was full of secrets, but joining forces with the single father was Kate's only hope to survive.

LISCNM0707